WEATHER EYE

LESLEY

HOWARTH

CANDLEWICK PRESS
CAMBRIDGE, MASSACHUSETTS

Also by Lesley Howarth:

The Pits

MapHead

Copyright © 1995 by Lesley Howarth

Second U.S. edition 1995

Library of Congress Cataloging-in Publication Data
Howarth, Lesley.
Weather eye / Lesley Howarth.— 1st U.S. ed.
Summary: In England in 1999, thirteen-year-old Telly
organizes her fellow climate observation club members
to calm the planet's turbulent weather.
ISBN 1-56402-616-7
[1. Weather—Fiction. 2. Natural disasters—Fiction.
3. England.—Fiction.] 1. Title.
PZ7.H83593We   1995
[Fic]—dc20   94-48918

2 4 6 8 10 9 7 5 3

Printed in the United States

Candlewick Press
2067 Massachusetts Avenue
Cambridge, Massachusetts 02140

CONTENTS

U N D E R   T H E   S T O R M

All night long the wind blew. Northern hemisphere isobars were going ape — and how — on every forecast map. The sinister-looking weather front had swirled in from the mid-Atlantic. In the toe of southwest England, spit center under the storm, lay a lonely, moon-flooded moor. On the moor stood a windfarm. On the windfarm, tucked among the wind turbines like a cat in mint, stood a stone-faced, six-eyed house. In the second-largest bedroom upstairs, behind blue and green curtains she'd agonized over when her room had been redecorated, stood Telly's bed. In the bed Telly and Race huddled, listening. There was no doubt about it. Whoever ran the world's weather was out to lunch. No one did, of course. The weather ran itself. Or *had* done well enough, time out of mind, Mum said. Until about ten years ago. Things had been getting steadily worse ever since Telly could remember.

All night long the wind blew. It *would* be bad when Mum was away, thought Telly, feeling out anxiously through the storm with some part of herself for her mother. It felt like such a long way—there were three wind-lashed counties and most of Glamorgan between them. Mum was away on windfarm business in Wales. There was a lot more to running a windfarm than watching the turbines go around making easy power from the wind. Someone had to sell it. Mum always negotiated contracts. Sometimes finding a buyer for a year or two's supply of electricity took her a week or so, sometimes it took a lot longer. Dad made the power, Mum sold it; that was the way it worked. Telly pictured the wild Welsh hills and the wild, wet Welsh woods and valleys; and she knew that her mother lay listening and worrying under some wind-shivered roof just as she did.

Telly looked up. Her bedroom ceiling creaked ominously. Somewhere above, the wind banged and boomed in the rafters. Telly's ears throbbed. She could practically feel the change in air pressure as the wind shifted. Race hid his head under the quilt. How strong *was* the roof, wondered Telly. How bad would the next gust be? Bad enough, when it came. Telly and Race listened, holding their breath against each crisis with a how-much-worse-can-it-get clench in their too-tight, what-a-night chests. Telly was a Weather Eye, so of course, it concerned her. She swung out of bed and stumbled across to the window.

"Must be bad, the turbines've stopped." Telly looked out incredulously. "Must be force eight or nine. Gusting to ten, I should—"

Another blast slammed down on the house, rumbling it, shuddering it, reminding it how perky and toothsome it was with its sky dish and chimney, how downright cheeky in standing on South Hill at all when the wind might blow it away if it chose. *And tonight it might,* thought Telly, *tonight it might* just *choose.*

"Gusting force ten over Pell Mell, I should think," she finished soberly. They both listened, waiting for the worst. What *was* the worst, wondered Telly?

"What if the house blows down?" asked Race in a small voice.

"We're up against the chimney stack," Telly reassured him. "Strongest part of the house."

Race stared up at the bedroom ceiling. "What if the chimney fell down on us, Telly?"

Telly considered. "What if it didn't."

"I don't like the wind," whimpered Race. "Feels like it's going to bang in the windows or something."

Telly looked at her brother. Still occupying most of her bed into which he'd propelled himself an hour ago, and laying in the same position he'd landed in, he looked seriously small and frightened.

There was no way he'd go back to his own room while the storm lasted. He was only eight, after all. He probably thought it was the end of the world or something.

"Something's going on, isn't it?" whispered Race. "Isn't it, Telly?"

"Like what?"

"You know. With the weather. It never used to, did it?"

"Be like this?" Telly brought her curtains together tightly. "It's only a storm. It'll blow itself out."

"But it's getting worse, isn't it?" persisted Race. "Worse than what it was."

Telly struggled with herself. It *was* worse, of course; even their grandparents, last to acknowledge change of any kind, had opened the subject on the weekend. But could she open it to Race?

"Okay, it *is* getting worse," she conceded. "That's why I'm doing Weather Eye."

"Weather Eye's rubbish. S'only a lame kids' club."

"Least we know what's going on," said Telly sharply. "Least we *talk* about it."

Race turned his back and pressed his forehead to the wall. He could feel the wind bounding in the chimney all the way down through the stonework. The sound of it filled his stomach.

Telly watched Race thoughtfully. It would be a mistake to let him know how frightened she was herself. Far from an open book, he was almost as obscure as Race Peters, the never-seen Australian uncle he was named after. But Telly's brother didn't need the bush to go walkabout. Race went walkabout in his head. That was his problem. He thought too much.

Telly softened her voice. "Want to go in with Dad?"

Race shook his head.

"Then pass me my Eye wallet, will you?"

Race fumbled between the bed and the wall and passed it. Telly flipped on her light and seated herself at her desk under the window. The window rattled threateningly.

The curtains breathed in and out with the wind, alternately puffing and plastering against the glass, dragging on the sill with an itchy sound more unsettling, somehow, than the suck of the storm outside. *I'll huff*, thought Telly, *and I'll puff. And I'll blow your house down. What then?* She wondered how Mrs. Ruddock was getting on. Neighbor Mrs. Ruddock occupied the eastern end of the house. She was probably in bed, deaf to the world. She was pretty deaf, anyway.

Telly opened her black nylon wallet with the "Eye" logo staring out top right. The Weather Eye symbol was a white eye with a rain cloud eyebrow and a green and blue Earth for a pupil. Telly'd been a fully fledged Weather Eye for almost six months.

Her name and address on the Official Membership Card—Teresa Louise Craven, The Windfarm, South Hill, Pell Mell—had her secret code name underneath, plus Eye Network Passwords for the computer bulletin board, regional Weather Hotlines, and all the other keys she was privy to since joining.

Telly drew out a Trauma Report. She clicked her Eye Reporter pen. First she entered the date: 18 October 1999. Then the time on her radio alarm clock: 4:10 A.M. Then she considered the Event Ratings. Checking off Wind Trauma firmly, she gave it a rating of ten. Wind direction? Telly opened the window a crack. Race moaned and humphed the quilt over his head. Telly shut the window. She listened intently. Then she wrote "Westerly." Duration? Six hours to time of report. Local effects? Telly tapped her pen on her braces. Local effects would have to wait until daylight.

She closed the wallet thoughtfully. Another six months' observation and she'd qualify for Accredited Air Monitor status. The wind boomed in the roof. The desk light blinked and faltered. Then it went off and stayed off. *Power lines down somewhere,* thought Telly. She flipped open her report again and held it under the window, entering an Impingement Factor 7—Disruption of Local Services.

Race had subsided under the quilt. Telly got up and pressed her face against the window, feeling the wind thundering over the glass outside, making out the sleekly tapered windmills, or turbines, dotting the hill in the moonlight, their long arms fixed and unmoving. The thick white shaft of the nearest turbine neatly bisected her view. It was unsettling to see them idle. Usually their steady, swishing rotation was as much a part of home as the cat washing its leg beside the fire. But tonight—incredibly—the wind turbines were still. It had to be storm force ten. Any hint of a tenner and they cut out automatically, as the strain became too great for the braking system that kept them turning day in, day out, at a constant thirty-five revolutions per minute. They would cut in again when the wind became more civil. It was only the second time in her life Telly had seen them idle.

Suddenly Race sat up. "What about Dewie?"

"What about Dewie? Dewie's okay."

"He might blow over. He did before."

"He's got bricks on his hutch, remember? It can't blow over now."

"He'll be frightened."

"He's a rabbit," said Telly flatly. "He'll be fast asleep in his hay."

Race swung his legs out of bed. "I'm going out to get him."

"Don't be stupid. You can't go and get him now."

Race got up. Swiftly, Telly moved between her brother and the door. "I'll get Dad," she warned.

Race rubbed his eyes. He was trembling. "I want Dewie."

"He'll be fine. You'll see he's fine in the morning."

"He won't be an' I *want* him."

Race set his jaw. There was no reasoning with him when he was like this. Telly sighed. "If you get back in bed, I'll go and check on Dewie. But you owe me."

"*And* bring him in."

"So where's he going to go?"

"In my room so's he's safe."

Telly pointed Race back into bed. "In. And don't get out till I come back. No matter what, all right?"

Race climbed meekly under the quilt. Just after Telly went out he called her back.

"Telly?"

Telly looked round the door. "What?"

"Mind they don't get you."

"Who don't get me?"

Race hesitated. "The Drafts."

Telly grinned. "I'll be quick."

Race turned over in bed. He'd been frightened of drafts since he was small. He knew it was silly— now—but in his weaker moments, they gripped him. The Drafts had grown in his mind into half-formed monsters from a warning half-understood. "I'll close the door, or the draft'll come in." His mother's voice had echoed in the corridor at bedtime all down the years since he was small. Still did. It was part of an unchanging ritual. "I'll close the door, or the draft'll come in. I'll leave the hall light on, all right?" Close the door. Keep out the drafts. Race had grown careful to keep his door closed. Darkness was preferable to drafts. After a while, Race came to know what Drafts looked like. They had vague, dark bodies and faces like owls. They scuffled in corners, quivering with malice, waiting for their chance to slip in. He must keep them out at all costs. They seemed to be everywhere, even the living room. "Shut the door," his mother would complain, by the fire. "That draft comes in like a knife."

Telly drew on her wellies by the howling back door. The draft cut under it, making the edge of the mat flop like a live thing. She zipped up her coat. Race and his stupid Drafts. He should worry, tucked up cozy in bed. The wind raged outside the door like an animal big enough to eat Drafts for breakfast. Telly hesitated, feeling for the flashlight on the windowsill. It wasn't there. Telly bit her lip. The moon was out. It would be light enough to see in. She would dash out, squint into Dewie's hutch, and dash back. She probably wouldn't get him. Dewie was large and stubborn. He had big back legs like a chicken that could deliver a spiteful kick.

Telly opened the door. The wind sucked her out and stuck all her hair onto her face. The treetops roared. Somewhere, something was banging. She shut the door during a lull like a vacuum and turned to face the path. Mum's vegetable patch looked weird. The heavy-headed sprout plants were smashed in shapes so strange they looked like seaweed from hell. The wind funneled up the path, filling Telly's coat as if it were inflatable. It was a warm wind. Heavy, powerful, freakish. It wanted to press her down and lift her up in the same moment.

A rumble grew in the treetops. Telly's hair lifted, wandered, waited. Strangely speeded-up clouds raced across the moon. The wind blustered in push-me–pull-you vortices, way up in the intricate sky. Telly's hair settled, ever so lightly, on her cheek. The heavens shifted, swayed, and burst, roaring down like a wave. The back door flew open violently. The wind rushed in, lifting the coats on their pegs in hectic gestures, rifling the phone book, skating the cat's bowl over the kitchen floor like a Frisbee. Telly fought the door, dragged it home, latched it firmly behind her this time. What a night! Enough to blow the cows home—who was it who said that? Dad. "Enough to blow the cows home on their own," Dad said. And *that* was at nine o'clock.

The nearest wind turbine stood two hundred yards or more down the slope. Telly could hear its thrumming plainly as she battled down to Dewie's hutch. The noise was unearthly. All the turbines were singing in the wind like a tuneless comb-and-tissue band as the gale cut through their finely angled edges. The nearest turbine dwarfed her as she approached it, like an awful giant she knew very well but couldn't entirely trust. Its thirty-meter-high shaft vibrated threateningly all the way up to the square-shaped cabin at the top. The spinner, or hub, attached to the cabin buzzed nastily. Locked in position, the three mighty sword-shaped blades radiating from it had taken up the note. The whole structure sang like a beehive. From its base to the tip of its blades, a forty-five-meter-high beehive—right over Telly's head.

The underground cables beneath her carried no charge tonight. Usually they fed the greedy grid with enough power from the turbines to light up three thousand homes. But tonight the windfarm was down. So was the National Grid—at least as far as Pell Mell. The village lights were absent. *We're out, they're out—tit for tat,* thought Telly.

"Dewie, you nerd. Where are you?" Telly scanned the rabbit's run. Of course, he wasn't in it. He would be in the closed-in sleeping compartment of his hutch on a night like this.

Every other day, Race dragged Dewie's hutch and run onto new grass. Dewie moved in a clockwise direction around the base of the turbine nearest the house. By the time he reached the position where the hutch had started, the grass had recovered. Dewie traveled in a wide arc. *Just as well,* thought Telly, *considering his appetite.* He'd gotten into the garden once and slaughtered the spring lettuce. Once he went to the pub. Race had left his hutch open accidentally, and Dewie had gotten out. They searched all the usual places, but he wasn't found till the next evening, when he was spotted sitting coolly outside the pub a mile and a half down the road. Dewie's Big Adventure was a well-worn family joke. Fill up his bottle with beer, joked Dad. Give him a taste of what he's missing. Ask him if he likes his vodka straight up. *Ha,* thought Telly. *Ha.* Where was he now, Dewie the Booze, when she wanted a sight of him most? She opened his hutch with difficulty. Hay dust huffed up in her face. *Hurry,* blustered the sickly, warm wind, the roaring trees, and the scudding, fast-forward sky. *Hurry,* whined the turbine overhead. Anything! Could happen!

Upstairs in bed Race turned a page of his *Animal Atlas.* His head was tingling. The only reason he was reading was to keep himself from jamming his head out of the window to see what was going on. Telly and Dewie. Dewie and Telly. Outside in the howling animal-wind. Because of him. He hunkered down and turned another page. "The panda is a shy vegetarian," he read. "It munches its way through about six hundred bamboo stems every day and spends most of its time just eating. Baby pandas are blind and helpless when they are born in the misty mountain forests of southwest China—"

Whuff, hit the wind on the house. Race sat up. Someone shouted. Dad, wasn't it? He jumped up and opened the window. A single flashlight beam wandered between the turbines. Briefly, it danced on Dewie. Or rather, Dewie's hutch.

Telly looked up. Dewie squirmed away from her clutching hand as the flashlight beam found her. Dad! Dad with the flashlight, emerging from the turbine tower by the hedge, securing the cubicle door behind him, checking things over with a querulous spot of fractured yellow light that slipped and slid over the ground, the hutch, her shoulders, the ground again— returning, incredulously, to find her.

"Telly!" bawled Pat Craven. "Get back inside!"

Telly straightened. "Just checking Dewie! We thought he might be frightened!"

The flashlight beam grew as her father approached. "Storm force eleven, for God's sake . . ." A rush in the trees. Everything lifted and thrummed as the wind threw her father's words in the sky. "I don't know what you think you're . . . GET IN NOW!"

Telly shut the hutch with the drum of blood in her ears. The booming wind lifted a horrible panic in her belly. Storm force eleven. No wonder. Her father's widening flashlight beam searched the shaft of the turbine above her. A snickering buzz had set in some-where along its length, rising nastily with the muscu-lar rumble of the storm.

"Get away from that turbine!" Pat Craven broke into a run. The air was electric. Danger, so thick you could lick it. "I don't like the sound that one's mak-ing! Telly! GET AWAY!"

Race saw it happen. Clear as day in the moonlight, half-in, half-out of the window. He saw the cladding of the turbine blade peeling down like banana skin. Fifteen meters of precision-molded fiberglass twisting in the moonlight like a pearly fish on a line. He heard the disaster-movie sound it made; he saw the half-a-blade hanging; he saw it whipped from its hub. And he saw it fall on Telly.

2

T H E   T R E E   I N

T H E   M E A D O W

Telly was looking down on herself. Everything was still. She could see herself quite plainly. Her father lifted her up. "Telly," he said. "Oh, Telly." *Poor Dad,* she thought, *poor Dad. I wouldn't be him for the world.*

She was somewhere above him in the air. Somewhere calm and still. She could see herself below, lying on the ground by the rabbit hutch with a no-one-at-home roll to her oddly absent eyes. She could see the shattered strip of cladding that must have struck her down. Just below her to the right, so close she could make out the bird droppings streaking it, she could see the roof of the cabin at the top of the turbine, thirty meters up, which she'd never seen before. *How strange,* she thought. *How strange.* Near, yet far, she saw her father search her eyes for signs. She saw him fumble her neck for a pulse. She felt strangely unconcerned.

Her father tilted her neck. He closed her nose with his fingers. He looked up once, with an awful look. Telly welled with pity. Not for herself, but for him. Then he plunged on her mouth—one time, two times, three. He watched along her belly. Her stomach rose and fell. He tilted her neck some more, sobbing his broken breath in her mouth. Telly became more distant. She saw her father howling soundlessly in the wind for help. She saw Race bolt from the house to join him. She saw her father crying, as if from a great height. Then the scene seemed tiny, as though she were viewing it down the wrong end of a telescope. And then she was alone in a tunnel.

A long, dark, enclosing tunnel. She was rushing along it in a tremendous burst of exhilaration. At the far end, something waited. Something wonderful. It was a light and not a light. It was everything she'd ever wanted. She yearned along towards it, and the tunnel helped her go. She wanted the light, and the light wanted her. Together, they would be perfect. She burst through in a warm rush that lit her up like a sun. A warm, wide meadow enclosed her. Across the lovely meadow a glorious, all-knowing tree spread its arms in delight. Beyond wanting, she wanted the tree; and the tree wanted her. She floated across the meadow, and the meadow lifted her up. Once she reached that glorious tree, she knew she would never turn back.

Then she remembered Race. She remembered poor old Dad, breaking his heart by the hutch. How would they manage without her? What would Mum do, if she went? In the moment she remembered, the light and the meadow were gone. She was falling back in darkness at a million miles an hour. The tunnel walls rushed past so fast she glimpsed imploding stars. The roughhouse sky, the puckered moor, the house, the bird-streaked turbine—all rushed toward her so fast they made her feel bad; just about as bad as she'd ever felt in her life. Her head had been stamped on—hadn't it? She could hardly breathe—cough, why don't you? *Cough.*

"Good girl," said Dad. "And another."

Telly heaved and coughed. A big dry cough that brought up something sicky. Then she opened her eyes. Dad looked down with a naked face. Behind him, Race broke a smile. Still smiling, he started to cry. He looked pretty silly, thought Telly, with the wind cracking through his pajamas and smears of wet down his cheeks. Dewie jumped in his hutch. The turbine above them sang in the wind, a different song now, through its stripped and shattered blade. Her father gathered her up. "Thank God," he was saying, "thank God." He said it over and over and over, with a funny catch in his voice.

"It hurts," said Telly.

"It will," said Dad, cradling her up the path.

"You've taken a knock on the head. But you're all right now, we'll fix it."

No, thought Telly, *you don't understand. The wonderful tree. It hurts so much to leave it.*

The emergency room at six in the morning was something else. Hospital business was brisk.

WELCOME TO THE EMERGENCY ROOM said the electronic information board over the central desk. KEEP ENTRANCE BAY CLEAR. HAVE YOU PAID AND DISPLAYED?

Hospital radio cut in over the reception area speakers with a list of early requests for Children's Wards 8 and 9. The Cravens didn't wait long. Just long enough to see an oldish man in a wheelchair finally get the cast cut off his knee after persistent, wistful complaints to passing nurses. "I can't get on with it. It's giving me grief," he told them. Telly wished him well. She saw he had fourteen years, five months, and three days left of his life. He might as well enjoy it.

Fourteen years. Five months. And three days. It was curious. The numbers popped up in her head. And that wasn't all she knew. Not by a long stretch. Since the glorious tree in the meadow, she knew there was nothing at all to be afraid of, not even the weather. And that was worth everything else twice over. Forget computer clubs, thought Telly, comfortably, in X-ray. Forget Air Monitor status. Forget

Trauma Reports. Forget fear of weather. Forget Weather Eye. Unafraid of anything, she *was* Weather Eye. That, and a whole lot more. She was in control. And Race?

Race had brought his *Animal Atlas*. He read with difficulty, jumping at every clunk on the wards, every bat of the doors. He sharpened up, with the X-rays. They sat on doughy red seats until the doctor swished out with the plates. They all considered Telly's perfect skull. The doctor showed them how, pointing up the way the radiographic plates collided to form an all-around picture.

A glowing picture of health, conceded the doctor. "She's a very lucky girl, Mr. Craven. No sign of any fractures. But we'd like to keep her in for observation."

"No!" Telly jumped. "There's too much to do."

Dad's face flickered. "There's nothing to do. Calm down."

"She might be in shock," said the doctor, over Telly's head.

"I'm not." Telly locked eyes with the doctor, who was young, with feather-cut hair. "I'll stay in bed. I'm all right."

"Telly, listen. This is serious." Pat Craven took her hand. "You stopped breathing. I thought—I thought you were dead."

I was, thought Telly. *Sort of. But then I decided not to be.* "I saw you when I was up in the air," she said.

"When you were up in the air?"

"I saw you giving me the kiss of life. I was up in the air by the turbine. Then I went through a long, dark tunnel with a light at the end. There was a lovely field and a tree. But I knew if I reached the tree I'd never come back. I thought about you and Mum and Race. Then I opened my eyes and I was lying on the ground and you and Race were there and everything hurt all over."

The doctor stirred. "Sounds like an NDE."

"A what?" asked Telly's father.

"A Near Death Experience," murmured the doctor. "More common than you might think." She turned to Telly crisply. "We're lucky to have you back. You might feel all right now, but we need to make sure you stay all right. Just for twenty-four hours."

"I *will* stay all right. I'll stay all right at home."

Feather-cut drew Pat Craven aside. "Perhaps we might talk in my office. This might have repercussions."

Pat Craven frowned. "Repercussions?"

"Behavioral changes, perhaps. Seeing yourself dead. It's quite an experience."

"Wait here," said her father, to Telly. "There's a *Smash Hits* over there in the rack."

Telly and Race waited. People came and went. Race watched everyone carefully to see what was wrong with them all. Some people looked quite normal, but that was only because they had some disgusting disease or other you couldn't see. The ones who looked OK were the worst. Race warmed to those with obvious injuries. They were lucky. They'd get Gatorade and comics and weeks and weeks in bed. Hospital radio played a chart entry for Anna in Ward 9. Keep your chin up, from all at Vale Road Primary. Then they played an old Madonna—"Holiday"—something for young Christopher Anthony in Children's Ward 8 to look forward to when he went home next week. Can't wait for the day, ran the message. All our love, Granny Williams. *"Holiday—it would be so nice,"* sang the radio. Then it gave way to local news.

"Extensive structural damage in the wake of last night's storms has meant a full schedule for local emergency services, with major roads closed in much of the Southwest due to flooding," announced the newsreader. "In South Wales, emergency crews have fought through the night to restore essential services. Residential parks near the southern Cornish coast have been devasted by winds gusting up to a hundred and ten kilometers an hour in some places. Electricity supplies have been disrupted over a wide area, with some villages facing a cut-off of up to thirty-six hours. And in a fall that was heard in neighboring Mount Oak, the famous three-hundred-year-old Wizzen Tree on the summit of Bready Lookout came crashing down in the early hours of the morning. With further storms expected, drivers are advised to avoid non-essential journeys. Over now to weatherman Russell Gammy."

Race slipped a mint into his mouth. He offered one to Telly. But Telly shook her head, listening now to the forecast. Not a bright lookout, from the sound of it.

"Not much comfort from me, I'm afraid, Jim," took up Russell Gammy cozily. "Batten down the hatches is the message from the weather center, with last night looking very much like a taste of things to come. This powerful, rather turbulent low pressure area we're experiencing will deepen over the south-west, keeping us very much on our toes over the next few days, bringing with it, I'm afraid, all that unpleasant, rather blustery weather we've come to expect from these sudden continental systems sweeping in without much warning. You'll need to keep those umbrellas handy with not much to shout about on the satellite picture until Wednesday brings a slight lift over much of the south. In the meantime, keep a weather eye out for sudden showers likely over western areas as we won't be seeing much letup rainwise until nearer the end of the week—"

"Come on," said Telly, "*I'm* Weather Eye."

"What d'you mean?" asked Race.

"There's no time for this. Come on."

"Where?" asked Race. "Why?"

"Because," said Telly grimly, "things are getting worse."

Telly approached the desk. The receptionist looked up. "Can you tell Mr. Craven, Miss Craven will see him at home?" asked Telly politely. "She's sorry she couldn't wait."

The receptionist threw Telly a bored look through outsize glasses with bright red frames. "Mr. Craven?" she queried, flatly.

"He's seeing the doctor now."

"And you are?"

"Elspeth Hymes," said Telly glibly, picking a class-mate she didn't like much. "I was sitting next to Miss Craven. Miss Craven had to go home."

The receptionist made a note on her pad. She transferred a call on her switchboard. She didn't look up again. Telly turned away. She looked at Race. Then she slipped out through the heavy double doors.

Race watched her go. He placed his Snoopy bookmark carefully in his *Animal Atlas*. He looked around him vaguely. YOUR DUTY NURSE TODAY IS WENDY WATKINS, said the electronic information board. WAITING TIME LIMITED TO THIRTY MINUTES SUBJECT TO EMERGENCIES. PLEASE BE A PATIENT PATIENT. Race stood up. No one told him not to. He checked his watch by the clock on the wall. 6:45 A.M. precisely. He tucked his *Animal Atlas* into his anorak. Then he followed Telly.

"Why are you different?" asked Race.

"Who's different?" Telly depressed the clutch and changed up to third. The car lurched as the clutch bit. Then she saw there were lights up ahead. No worries. Clutch, and back to second. Or possibly straight down to first, why not? As long as she kept the clutch pressed down, nothing too bad could happen with the gears. Nothing too bad could happen to them anyway, thought Telly. Race, she could see, had seventy-nine years, two months, and thirteen days more of his life stretching ahead of him, and she had—slow down *now,* clutch and brake together. Nothing to it. And she had—she had flip knew *how* many years to go. Lots of them, anyway. So there you were. Nothing much could happen, no matter what she did. Surprising how easily driving came, once you'd got up the courage. There was nothing to be afraid of. That was the joke. Even when you finally reached the end of the road, the wonderful meadow was waiting.

"*You're* different. Why are you?" repeated Race.

Telly thought. "The difference is, I'm not afraid," she said simply. "I'm not afraid of anything at all."

Race swallowed. "Not even Drafts?"

"Especially not Drafts," said Telly.

Race folded his hands in his lap. "You shouldn't drive fast, Telly."

"I shouldn't drive at *all*. Going good though, aren't I?"

"What about Dad? He'll be hopping mad we left him at the hospital."

"He won't be a happy bunny," conceded Telly.

"Why did we leave him at the hospital?"

"Because we had to." Telly sighed. "He'll probably grab a bus. Probably beat us home. I couldn't stay in the hospital. Not with this system blowing in."

"I don't like systems either," said Race, without a clue to what they were. "Lights're going green."

Telly pulled away. Lots of accelerator, then lots of clutch. Straight from first gear to third. "This weather system coming in from the west's going to be a biggie—"

"How d'you know?"

"I just *do*. Which way shall we go? Bypass, or main road through town?"

"Not around town," said Race. "I'm tired."

Telly watched him. He was. His eyes looked red and puffy. He'd had a lot of upset and very little sleep, remembered Telly. She'd better get him home and tuck him up in bed. Then she would get to work. So much to do, so little time.

She managed fourth gear on the bypass. Race dozed off in his seat. The sense of speed and freedom on the open, empty road with the roaring trees in the hedges stretching away before her was better than anything Telly had ever felt before in her life. She could almost taste it. It tasted of early morning. Soon the spidery wind turbines near the horizon thickened into home. She turned off at Three Lanes, wending through Holes and Rudda, coasting right at Black

House on the Pell Mell road. The giant tips of the turbine blades seemed to follow the car above the ridges like the lances of some hidden army. As they took the Pell Mell turn the moor opened before them, throwing the gleaming white windfarm and the orange dawning sky straight in Telly's face. It was a beautiful new day. The best day Telly'd seen. Whatever the weather threatened, she was more than equal to it. In this new day nothing could touch her. In this new day she *was* Weather Eye.

3

HOME ALONE

Race mixed his mixture thoughtfully. The hall bonged dolefully with the force of the wind outside. The storm continued unabated; nothing outside had changed much since last night; plenty inside had. Telly, for instance. Telly had been closeted in her room with the computer—the electricity had been on again when they'd gotten back—for the last half-hour or so, following the fight they'd had over Race going to bed. Or *not* going to bed. No way was he going to bed at breakfast time—what did she think?

In his bowl on the hall step Race mixed the insides of one tea bag, a bit of flour, a pinch of salt and sugar, a teaspoon of coffee—ground, not instant—and a little bit of water. As he mixed, he thought. He thought about everything that had happened. After a while he got up off the step and fetched the bulging photo box from underneath his mother's side of the bed. He wished she'd come back from her business trip. He guessed she soon would, once she heard what had happened.

Race cocked his head. Footsteps out on the path. A clump at the letterbox. It was only Greville Jackett. Greville Jackett, out delivering papers in the worst storm this century. *That'd be right,* thought Race. *Super Paper Boy.* Nothing but hell itself opening under him would stop Greville Jackett from delivering the papers. The *Western Morning Herald* introduced itself rather rudely through the letter-box and plopped onto the hall floor. Race picked it up. STORMS DEVASTATE WEST screamed the headline. WIDESPREAD DISRUPTION AS MINI HURRICANE HITS. Race was about to frisbee the paper into the kitchen when a small paragraph at the bottom of the front page caught his eye. "Great Balls of Fire" read the header. Race was intrigued. He read on:

Westcountry stargazers could witness fireworks in the sky tonight as the Earth crosses the orbit of a disintegrating comet. Astronomers say that the comet Fleet-Hibble, likely to be the closest ever to approach the Earth, should make impressive viewing. The best time to spot it in the northwestern sky should be between 11:00 P.M and 12:00 P.M. In past centuries comets were feared as heralds of disastrous events.

Race repeated the last sentence to himself, catching the gist, if not every word. It sounded exciting.

Fireworks in the sky. He would have to make sure he stayed up. He flipped the paper onto the hall table and checked the brown mixture in his bowl. He poked it a bit. It was firming up nicely. He fetched a cushion from the living room and plumped it onto his step. Then he turned his attention to the photo box. Upending it over the floor, he spilled the story of his life over the hall tiles.

Upstairs in her bedroom, Telly sat back. She called up OPTIONS and changed the screen environment to green. Then she changed it to blue. Better. The computer blindly offered format options against a brilliant blue background until she hit RETURN. Then it flashed up a central box: To Page Bulletin Board Use Any Key. Telly hit an M. Then she keyed in her personal Eye Network Password. Her freshly composed message winked up. SENDING pulsed the box at the top right-hand corner of the screen. Usually she bypassed Privileged Sending Options, but she wanted an overwrite on this one. This was important. Her message would overwrite the usual Bulletin Board exchange of information for two minutes precisely. It was going out to Weather Eye Club members everywhere at this very moment. It wasn't much, but it was a start. There would be three messages. This was the first.

Telly hit ESCAPE, exiting rapidly through a word processing environment largely created by her mother. Then she called up the directory. A list of file names prefixed by MAG appeared. Telly's mother's name was Maggie. She fronted all her files with the first three letters of her name. Snooping, Telly optioned subdirectory MAG.WHINE. A list of files popped up, headed by MAG.PIDDLE and MAG.STINK. Telly grinned. She knew about MAG.PIDDLE and MAG.STINK. They headed a long list of complaints. MAG.PIDDLE was a strident letter to the local water company dating from the time their water had turned yellow. MAG.STINK was a letter to the *Herald* about car exhaust pollution. An active campaigner on environmental issues, Maggie Craven never let up once she had the bit between her teeth. Telly shook her head. Mum. What a firebrand she was. When would she be back?

Downstairs in the hall Race had found what he was looking for. It was nothing but a careless snapshot showing a laughing brother and sister in sad holiday clothes. The sister was Race and Telly's mother, Maggie. The brother was their uncle, Race Peters. Race considered his namesake. One of Race Peters' long arms rested around his sister's shoulders, the other goosed her in the ribs. She laughed and held on to her hat. Race Peters laughed at her, laughing. They had the long, lean look of the Peters clan and a mouthful of teeth in common. Race turned the photo over. "Mags 'n' Race, Newquay, August '77," said the back. It had been taken the summer Race Peters had emigrated to Australia.

Race had never seen his antipodean uncle in the flesh. He'd heard the stories, though. Race Peters was a bit wild, from all accounts. Race guessed he was just about as different from his namesake as it was possible to be. Long, lean Race Peters. This was the only photo. Why had he dug it out now? Why was he thinking about an uncle he'd never even seen? He didn't really know. There were lots of things Race didn't know. Why had they left Dad at the hospital? Telly knew. He supposed it would all work out.

Race spread baby photos. He found a picture of himself in rolling cheeks and jowls and in most of the dirt by the back door. He could hardly believe it was him. The kid in the picture could hardly look over his cheekfat into the camera. His fatty legs were positively pneumatic. He looked as though he'd been pumped up with a bicycle pump. He must have been two, maybe three. It was just about then, thought Race. Just about then he'd started with the Drafts. Couldn't have been much before he was three, because he'd been in the old back bedroom before that, and the Drafts didn't know about him then. They'd only caught on to him when he moved bedrooms.

Tiring of photos, he swept them all up. He stuffed them every which way in the box. Then he shaped his mixture on the step. *Shape into desired shape,* thought Race, rehearsing *Make It With Race. Make It With Race* was an imaginary television program in which he demonstrated everything he did to credulous millions eager to learn the Race way with just about anything at all. *Add extra tea leaves if you want,* he advised his audience. *Roll it in flour two times to get effect. Then place in garden or on steps is good. Coil it up so it looks real.*

Race opened the back door. Holding the door with difficulty, he coiled his mixture carefully on the step. It was a real corker. Then he considered the storm outside. What about Dewie? He hadn't filled his feeder since the night before last. Dropping his mixing bowl, Race made for the garden shed and Dewie's bag of pellets.

Telly jumped when the phone rang. Dad. She felt muddled and sorry for leaving him, but it couldn't be helped. Not at all. She thundered downstairs and snatched up the phone on the fourth trill. "Pell Mell 839."

"Telly?" demanded the familiar voice. "What's going on? What are you doing at home?"

"I'm sorry, Dad. I couldn't stay in the hospital, I thought they'd make me and I—"

"Did you see the car? How on earth did you get home?"

Telly took a deep breath. "Mum left me money before she went," she heard herself saying. "There was a taxi outside the hospital." Both statements were true. It was just that they weren't connected.

"You took a taxi? But why?"

"I had to get away, Dad. Race was tired, I—"

"The thing is, the car's been stolen," broke in Pat Craven urgently. "I'm at Roadford Police Station now. As soon as I've finished here I'm hiring a car and—sorry? Thanks a lot. Just great. Telly? The Sergeant here says I can grab a lift home, so I'll not be long at all. Telly? Are you there?"

Telly swallowed. This, she hadn't considered. "The thing is—"

"Listen, you might not be feeling yourself. I want you to sit down in front of a video till I get back, and then I want to know what's going on. Is Race okay?"

"Race is fine. Dad, listen—"

"Got to go now. See you soon."

"Dad, wait—"

Dit. Dit. Cut off.

"The thing is, Dad . . . " Telly told the inattentive phone, "the thing is, I've got the car. I took the spare keys taped under the wheel arch. I drove it home all by myself. *It isn't stolen at all.*"

Footsteps pounded up the path. The back door imploded against the wall. Race skidded the length of the hall, meeting the living room carpet with a hiccup that threw him against the settee. He was wild and windswept and watery around the edges.

"Dewie's gone!" he wailed. "You never shut his hutch up!"

"Calm down." Telly tried to remember. "I might

not've. I only nearly got killed at the time. I might not've latched it properly."

"Come 'n' look," blubbered Race, "come 'n' look fr'im *now*."

Telly skirted the mess on the back doorstep. Race and his fake dog poo. She'd been caught one time too many with *that* one. Even so, it was hard to believe the step hadn't recently been visited by a dog with an urgent need to unburden itself. Race's fake poo was amazingly realistic. The coffee grounds were a masterstroke. They gave it just the right texture.

Telly followed her brother down to Dewie's patch. The wind had a different quality today. Lazy, but kind of heavier. It must have dropped, thought Telly. The turbines were turning again. Their rhythmic swishing whispered lies to Telly. Everything's—*swish*—all right. Everything's—*swish*—all right. Everything's—if only it were, thought Telly. She looked up. It was as though the atmosphere were stacked with lulls and flurries that sucked and tugged in no particular hurry. But the wheeling clouds above were something else. And the straining hilltops. Close to the ground the wind had sheathed its strength, for the time. But the sinister-looking sky promised more trouble than a cat in a bag.

The damaged turbine nearest the house dwarfed it by a gleaming, ivory-white mile. Telly caught her breath. No matter how many times she approached them, the turbines always awed her. It was difficult to grasp how very big they were. Over three times as high as the house, they had a presence all their own. In the full light of morning their slim and active lines made a contrast to the pylons which marched over the hill to meet them in a face-off of giants. The pylons weren't in the same league. They dumbly held up their power lines with their ugly latticed arms and had nothing much to say at all except: feet apart, arms out—we carry power lines, us. They were pretty much one-note wonders. But the wind turbines spoke of the future. They showed up the pylons for the clueless loadbearers they were. The turbines were stirrers. They were the shakers and movers of the century to come, bringing clean and effortless power to light up living rooms, charge computers, make radiant children's bedrooms.

The wind turned their blades, and the blades turned the spinner, and the spinner turned the drive shaft, way up in the square-shaped cabin behind the blades; and the drive from the drive shaft jumped through the gearbox to turn over the generator. With its spinning magnetic coils the generator made the electricity which traveled down the hanging cables in the tower to arrive at the hut at its base. In the hut was a transformer. The transformer digested the electricity and zapped it out through underground cables to the substation; and the substation sent it out, continuously, to anyone who needed it. It was simple, clean, friendly—and popular. Everyone loved wind turbines. In stately, silent rhythm a looming field of giants with their long blades wheeling around could take your breath away. People turned off the bypass just to watch them. And there were plenty to watch. The last ten years had seen the march of windfarms over the moor. Way in the far distance, the outlines of Crossways Windpark made matchstick shapes on the horizon. Telly narrowed her eyes. Crossways was busy, too.

Race reached Dewie's hutch. It was plainly vacant property. "See!" Race pointed accusingly. "It's open! He's prob'ly gone a mile!"

"Come away!" bawled Telly. "Don't go under that turbine!"

The safety cutout had switched off the turbine, but the damaged blade above Race yawed horribly in the wind. The strip of fiberglass cladding that had felled Telly, in another life, it seemed, lay twisted beside the hutch. Race backed away. Then he dashed past her with his hair on end to look in the vegetable patch.

Telly looked up at the turbine. *Yes*, she thought, *you got me. You got me a good one last night.* Everything was coming to pieces like the stripped and broken blade. Mum was away. Dad was stranded. Race was desperate. Dewie had gone where bad rabbits go. The storm was gathering, with the Big One yet to come. *Good thing I got back when I did*, thought Telly.

Not a moment too soon. Good thing things were in hand. She smelled the air. It smelled dangerous. She had a feeling Dewie's escape was the least in a long list of worries.

Telly turned and followed Race. Then she did a double take. A large nightdress of indeterminate shape decorated the windward side of the garden wall. Its arms appealed for help with every flip of the wind. Telly stared. The helpless nightdress was more unsettling, somehow, than just about anything else. *Mum*, she thought. *Where are you? What are you doing today?* Telly felt tears rising. She swallowed them back. Weather Eyes didn't have tears. Stretching away down the right-hand side of the slope a trail of large, flesh-colored underwear flagged the gap in the hedge where the rest of Mrs. Ruddock's washing had been flung away by the storm. Telly peeped through. The wind had been even-handed with the smaller items. A host of colorful tea towels checkered the field beyond.

After they'd searched the vegetable patch for any hole or cranny large enough to harbor the truant Dewie, Telly and Race struck out on the Pell Mell road. He might have gone to the pub, insisted Race. He might've remembered the way. Telly had sighed, and conceded. It was a bit of a gamble, in more ways than one. The wind shrieked over the moor. At least the Cornish hedges on the narrow village road offered some kind of bluff protection. Over against the far boundary of stony Foghanger Farm the moorland sheep huddled in a grubby, white lump against the outbuildings. The Fishbones were bringing them in. Telly jumped for a better view. She recognized the elder Fishbone by his ever-present hat, with a couple of circling dogs. Bringing in moorland sheep! *Things must be bad,* thought Telly.

"Why couldn't I come in your room?" complained Race. "What've you been doing?"

"Sending a message," shouted Telly, against the wind. "Weather Eye's different now. I'm changing it."

"What's different about it, then?" asked Race after a moment.

"Weather Eye? It's better." Telly paused. "More fun."

"What's fun about it?"

"We're all getting together to change things. Weather Eye's cool. You don't know."

Race digested this. Then he said, "Who's in it?"

"The Fishbones are. Denny and Helen."

"They would be." Race was unimpressed. "Who else?"

"Oh, loads," said Telly carelessly. "I'll show you a membership printout. Italy, France, New Zealand, Australia—"

"All over the world?" Race looked at his sister.

Telly nodded. "All over the world. Keeping an eye on the weather. And now it's going to change."

"What is? Weather Eye?"

"No," said Telly, "the weather."

They battled around a blind bend with the wind full in their face. The power lines running parallel to the hedge hummed a bitter song as the wind scoured through. There was something else, too. Something faint as angels, wafting down from the village. Telly hitched her hair behind her ears. Church bells, surely. She wondered why. It wasn't even Sunday.

"I'll be in it," said Race suddenly. "I want to be one."

"One what?"

"A Weather Eye."

"You can't," said Telly coldly.

"Why not?"

"You'd spoil it."

"Why?" asked Race.

"Because you're afraid," said Telly.

Race brooded. His indignation rose. "Am not," he said after a while.

"Are."

"Not."

"Oh," said Telly cuttingly, "you're not afraid of Drafts?"

"I don't care," bridled Race, "I'm bein' *in it*."

"Not unless I show you how. And I'm not about to do that."

"I'm not afraid of anything *else*."

"You can't be a Weather Eye unless you're not

afraid of anything at all, because that's how I'm changing it," said Telly. "Anyway. You don't follow the weather."

"I do, an' I'm—"

"Keep *in*, will you? We can't hear what's coming."

"—not scared of *anything!*" Race swaggered out in the road. "I can do this look, I c'n walk around—"

"Race!"

"—bends, an' I'm not even a weensy bit—"

The police car braked and swerved in the same moment, mounting the hedge, tilting along it on two screaming wheels and a wing, smashing down with horrible force in a fist of shattered glass. Race watched, fascinated, as the rear end of the car swiveled around to meet him in slow motion. Instead it met the hedge on the opposite side of the lane with a bang of metal on stone that brought everything, finally, to a jarring, horror-show halt. A moment later a large rock clunked out of the hedge. It rocked unhurriedly to a standstill.

Pat Craven exchanged a look with the police officer at the wheel. Then he climbed slowly out of the only undamaged door with an expression on his chalk-white face that neither Telly nor Race could remember having ever seen before.

4

THE HEROD

"The general synopsis at one three double-o: There are warnings of severe gales in Bailey, Faeroes, and southeast Iceland. Low, near southwest Iceland 982, slow-moving and filling 988 by one three double-o tomorrow. Low, German Bight, slow-moving, southeast, with little change. New developing low, moving steadily northeast, and expected one hundred and fifty miles west of Rockall one thousand and twelve by that time. Now the area forecast for the next twenty-four hours . . ."

The shipping forecast droned on behind clamorous teatime noises. No one was really listening, but it kind of leaked in through the skin. The familiar litany of place names—Rockall, Malin, Bailey—had a mournful sound today. Things were pretty wild at sea, thought Telly, setting the table.

"Thirteen of 'em," said Dad, thoughtfully stirring

bolognese sauce. "Thirteen dairy cows, laid out in a row like sardines. Dead as doornails, the lot of 'em."

"Poor old things." Telly centered the Parmesan cheese between the salt and pepper. No reason not to be orderly, no matter what was blowing up outside. "How come they were all in a line like that?"

"They were going in for milking, four o'clock yesterday. Power line blew down on 'em as they were filing under it, fried 'em where they stood. Good job it wasn't five minutes later or boy Turnbull would've copped it as well. Mrs. Ruddock said you never saw anything like it."

"When did you see Mrs. Ruddock?"

"Just now." Pat Craven grinned. "I helped her bring in her underwear. Her washing was plastered all over Lane End Field, right up as far as the stables."

"Big, aren't they?"

"The stables?"

"No," said Telly wickedly, "Mrs. Ruddock's underwear."

"Tell school again," sang Race, from under the kitchen table.

"School's blown down," said Pat Craven obligingly. "That do for you?"

"Yes!" Race knotted his fists over his head.

"Plate glass all over the playground. Bicycle shed roof's gone, too. Looked pretty bad when I passed it."

"Drastic," beamed Race, cracking dry spaghetti.

"How long d'you think *I'll* be off?" asked Telly. "What did Mrs. Yardley say?"

"When she rang? School is closed until further notice. Something to do with the electrics."

". . . Viking, sou'west or west, gale force nine or ten, worsening. Forties, Cromerty, Forth: southwesterly, veering northwesterly for a time, nine, occasional ten. Tyne, Dogger, mainly southwesterly eight, variable. Fisher, southwesterly nine to gale ten. German Bight, Humber, variable . . ."

Dad raised his voice over the radio. "How are you feeling?"

"Me?" Telly shrugged. "I'm fine."

"I still don't understand why you felt you had to go so suddenly. I wouldn't have made you stay in the hospital if you didn't want to."

"No," said Telly, dipping a finger in the spaghetti sauce, "but the doctor would have."

"I'm still not sure you're all right." Her father shot her an anxious look. "Going off like that. I can't believe you did that."

"I left you a message."

"Really didn't want to stay, did you?"

"I haven't time," said Telly.

"And you didn't see anyone taking the car?"

"No," said Telly truthfully. "What you making, Race?"

Race looked up over his pile of dry spaghetti.

"Jus' like, a spaghetti bridge you c'n brum cars on if you want."

Propping a sheaf of spaghetti on Lego piers, Race licked his fingers. *Stick 'em down with spit,* he advised his imaginary audience. *Else all the ends fall off.*

Pat Craven checked his saucepans. Then he watched Telly watching Race. "The doctor told me to bring you in with any marked change in behavior, you know," he told her.

"I'm okay. Really. I'd tell you if I wasn't."

Dad looked doubtful. "I don't know. What's letting your brother walk down the middle of the road like that? Marked change of behavior, or what?"

Telly sighed. "I told you. It happened so quickly."

"Everything's happening quickly," complained Pat Craven. "One minute everything's fine, then this storm blows up, there's your accident, the car's stolen—from a hospital parking lot—I'm coming home in a police car, find my son in the middle of the road. Constable said the police car's a write-off. Pretty calm about it, really. Good job I'm not being billed for that one." Pat Craven shook his head. "Stolen. From a hospital parking lot. I don't know what your mother's going to say."

Telly looked away. Dad was worried about the car. She longed to tell him it was up in Home Field. But that posed the horrendous problem of how to explain how it got there. It was an all or nothing kind of thing. She couldn't stop him worrying about the car without worrying him about something so much worse he'd be glad to worry about the car again. She hadn't thought about the consequences when she took it. Now she was in so deep it was difficult to front up with anything like the truth. *Hey, Dad. I drove the car home. Me. Yes. I drove it. It's behind the shed in Home Field. The car? I drove it home. With Race in it, yes. Without knowing how. On the bypass. Didn't I realize it was illegal? How dangerous it was? Kind of, I did. Didn't I realize I was endangering my own life and my brother's, not to mention everyone else's? The thing is, Dad, I wasn't. How did I know? I just did.*

Oh, that's all right, then. Fine. Tell me anytime you need the car again. Perhaps you'd like a personal set of keys?

Telly sighed and hooked out a chair from the corner. "Tea's ready." She gave Race a significant look. "Get out from under the table."

Race knew perfectly well the car was up in Home Field. He was only restrained from telling by dint of the enormous whopper Telly'd cooked up in a fierce whisper while Dad was helping bump-start the rubbished police car back up the lane. She knew where Dewie was. How did she know? She just did. If he said anything about the car or her driving it—anything at all—she wouldn't tell him *ever* and Dewie would go off and live with someone else. Someone who cleaned out his hutch more often. Where is he, then? Race had asked. You don't know where he is.

Don't I, though, taunted Telly. Drove the car back, didn't I? I saw him while you were asleep. Where? asked Race. Wouldn't you like to know, Telly had finished pointedly. Why didn't you say? persisted Race. Why were we going to the pub? Telly had stood crushingly, once, on his toe. Good thing he was only eight. Old enough to doubt himself, young enough to swallow what she said.

". . . Finisterre, northeasterly eight to gale nine, occasional ten," tolled the radio mournfully. "Sole, Lundy, Fastnet: southwesterly eight, worsening. Rockall, westerly eight, backing southerly and increasing nine or ten later. Malin, Hebrides: westerly eight or nine, occasional ten in the northwest. Bailey, southwesterly ten to storm force eleven, rain or showers, worsening. Fair Isle, Faeroes, southeast Iceland: south or southwest ten to storm force eleven, occasional hurricane force twelve in northwest, rain or showers, worsening—"

Pat Craven snapped off the radio. Then he strained the spaghetti over the sink, careful not to let it all slither and flump into the bowl of dirty dishes underneath, the way it had when Race had strained the spaghetti on the one and only occasion he'd insisted on doing it.

"Funny thing is . . ." he said thoughtfully, "funny thing is, I passed a lot of kids standing around, on the way home. Strange, really. Quite a few at Paynter's Cross. Just standing there, watching the sky. As if they thought something would happen."

It will, thought Telly. *And sooner than you think.* She helped herself to spaghetti, piling on bolognese sauce. Message received and understood. Weather Eye was really cooking now.

"Race," said Telly calmly. "Pass me the Parmesan."

At nine o'clock the meteors came. Or rather, they—and the Earth—came to the meteors. What they were seeing, explained Dad, was a long tail of dust and gas heated by the sun. The Earth was entering the orbit of the disintegrating comet Fleet-Hibble. The comet was called Fleet-Hibble after Mr. Fleet and Mr. Hibble, who had discovered it. Telly and Race ate salt and vinegar crisps on the living room windowsill as the horizon glowed in colors; colors so pretty-please pastel, so delicately draped on the night sky like veils, they reminded Telly of the floating, feather-heavy dresses of the waltzers on *Come Dancing*.

Race pleaded, and stayed up. By eleven the night sky was gorgeous. The tree line whipped and wagged against a light show high as the gods, melting with fuchsia pinks and minty, wandering greens.

"Let's go out," said Race, going out already.

The night was clear and wild. The wind barreled along the wall outside the back door, thrashing the potted plants one way, then the other. Several lay smashed under the windowsill. The trellis creaked;

an empty milk bottle rolled to and fro. Telly picked it up and jammed it by the door. Mrs. Ruddock's door opened. She joined them, wonderingly, on the stone-flagged terrace where the yucca plants rattled by the bins. Dustbins, noted Telly, that someone had weighted down with rocks. *So noisy and wild down here,* she thought; so cool and calm in the sky, where the mile-high colors glowed. The meteor shower was outside the weather. Outside everything. Way out there in the universe, nothing could blow out those lights.

Mrs. Ruddock looked up. "What is it?"

"Meteor shower," shouted Pat Craven. "Quite something, isn't it?"

"Hope it means a change in the weather," said Mrs. Ruddock vaguely. "Don't care for this wind much, do you? Sets your nerves on edge."

Pat Craven shook his head. "Must be force nine or ten, turbines keep cutting out. Forecast looks pretty grim. I'm losing money hand over fist."

"Where's the comet, then?" asked Telly, holding down her hair.

"This *is* the comet." Her father swept the sky with his arm. "We're traveling in its tail."

"Comets were once feared as herods of disastrous events," intoned Race. "What's 'herods'?"

"Come on," shouted Dad, "it's too windy. You can watch from your bedroom window."

"I'm not tired," said Telly.

"Come on, Telly. You must be."

"What's 'herods'?"

Dad focused on Race. Race looked blank. "What's 'herods'?" he asked again.

"What's he talking about?" Dad asked Telly.

Telly shrugged. "Search me."

"Heralds," shouted Mrs. Ruddock. "Heralds of disastrous events. The Light, you know. The Light at the End of the World."

Dad rolled his eyes, meaning Mrs. Ruddock might well have parted company with her trolley some considerable time since.

Telly grinned. "'Night, Mrs. Ruddock."

Mrs. Ruddock turned. "'Night, then, Telly. And Race."

Weather Eye lay on her bed and crossed her arms like an Egyptian mummy. Her thoughts rode the boom of the wind. She closed her eyes. If she listened hard enough, she could feel the knotted forces at the very heart of the storm. Six miles high in the jetstream where the knotty winds were born, something very big was out of kilter. It was a turbulent world, in more ways than one. Things were getting faster, more intense. Weather Eye could sense it. The boom of the wind said it all. You've gone and done it this time, thundered the weary world outside. How much did you think I could take? A million zillion car exhausts forever? Did you think I'd take it lying down? I'm here to tell you something better change.

In the bedroom next door Dad settled Race. Weather Eye could hear them talking plainly. Yes, Dewie's hutch was propped open. If he popped in during the night, the door would swing to behind him. If he was anywhere around, he would smell the cabbage Race had left out specially. Couldn't fail. He'd probably come back in the night and settle down like dandy in his hay. Race would find him fast asleep in the morning. They'd have a good hunt up the lane if he didn't. No, he wouldn't have gone far. Wasn't stupid, was he? Dewie knew on which side his bread was buttered. He knew a good home when he saw one.

Then the tone changed. "I don't know," said Dad. "What d'you think's going on?"

"The weather!" Race's voice was sharp. "You know what I mean!"

"Look, sometimes you get weather like this." Dad again, soothing. "It doesn't mean anything. We've had bad storms before. I remember staying off school because of the weather. We were cut off for three weeks in 1963. The Big Freeze, they called it. Snow in Granpa's lane high as the hedges." He paused, thinking. "I read somewhere they had snow in summer once, in eighteen twenty-something. The weather goes around and around. Just because it's stormy doesn't mean anything's going to hap —"

"Yes!" cried Race, "It does! The weather's funny, isn't it? Isn't it?"

A pause. "It's not so much that the weather's funny, it's just that—"

"It is funny!" Weather Eye could picture Race's angry face. "It's not like it normally is. Telly knows an' I know. Why can't you just say the weather's getting worse?"

Weather Eye waited. Why can't you? I know why you can't say it, she thought. It was because saying it made it real. She'd heard the soft-soap in Dad's voice when he talked about having had bad storms before. Race had heard it, too. Dad was being less than completely honest because he didn't believe what he was saying himself, not really. You can pretend there's been freak weather other times, thought Weather Eye. You can pretend all you like, but this time it's different. The kids can feel it. Adults can too, but they pretend they can't, all the same. That was the trouble with adults. There would be no adults in the Weather Eye Club, because they didn't want to see what was going on. There was another reason, too.

"It'll all blow over in a day or two," Dad was saying. "Just you wait and see. We'll get a new blade for that silly old turbine. Be up and running in no time. Warm enough in bed?"

The reason there wouldn't be any adults in Weather Eye was the same reason they couldn't admit, even to themselves, that there was something wrong with the weather. It was because they were afraid.

"Sleep tight, then," Dad told Race. "I'll pull the door to, keep out the draft."

"'Night, Dad!" called Weather Eye, the way Telly always did. "Can I ring Mum in the morning?"

"Yes," said Dad, "I want you to. But go to sleep now. Please."

He looked in and gave her a kiss. "No point mentioning what happened, as long as you feel okay. Not until Mum gets home, at least. Aren't you getting undressed?"

"In a minute," said Weather Eye. "'Night, Dad."

Weather Eye lay back. She felt her mind buzzing. She wasn't tired at all. The night was young, the wind was up. Anything! Could happen!

Taking out her notebook, she drew up her plan of action. Then she waited calmly in the still small center inside her for a very long time indeed. At 1:15 A.M. precisely, she put on her Weather Eye sweatshirt. By 1:30 A.M. she was revving the car in Home Field. The roads would be empty. Nothing would stop her. Once out on the lane, she adjusted the lights. Up for dim, down for full headlights. The glorious tail of Fleet-Hibble lit up the sky ahead. The Light at the End of the World, Mrs. Ruddock had called it. Weather Eye smiled to herself. End of Part One, more like. Nineteen ninety-nine, wasn't it? A special kind of year. The flourish at the end of two millennia. Beyond it lay all the things to come. Wonderful things. Weather Eye gripped the wheel. The comet Fleet-Hibble was no accident. It was a herod of glorious events. A bud of excitement blossomed inside her. She was sure of it.

Once out on the Cape Edge road, Weather Eye started to sing. She wound down the window and changed up to fourth. Loud and careless, smacked by cross winds, Weather Eye motored the lonely road that stretched away like a tunnel under the storm to fall at last off the Edge at the very last house in England.

5

T H E   E D G E

Drivers are advised, thought Telly. *Drivers are advised . . .* Who *was* that, up ahead? Weaving along in a tractor, at a quarter to two in the morning? *Drivers are advised . . . to avoid non-essential journeys.* Where had she heard that? The radio. The radio at the hospital, almost twenty hours ago. It seemed a lot longer. Anyway, this journey was more essential than most. Telly clicked on the car radio. Fuzzy Radio Cornwall filled the car. Funny the way the words of her message seemed to fit the music. Was it only hours ago she'd sent it?

STATUS CODE KAOS

PRIVILEGED OVERWRITE

Weather Eyes! Climatic conditions critical.
Outlook grim. Kids, brightening. Adults, dense
fog, little change. Global weather: out to

lunch, occasional hyper to severe. **THIS IS REAL.** Frightened when the wind blows at night? You should be. Something better change. Weather watchers everywhere. Get together. Watch this space.

Network Southwest: Meet Cape Edge, two a.m. tonight. If you dare. Something's going to happen. Message ends.

YOUR WEATHER EYE.

The message sang in Telly's brain, the way it had when she'd sent it pulsing out on the network that morning. It wasn't a bad message, considering she hadn't known quite what she was going to say when she wrote it. Bit woolly, perhaps—but that was feeling the future for you. How could she say what was going to happen until it happened? Weather Eyes everywhere would read her message. It would strike a chord with some. There would be another, more pointed, message tomorrow. It all depended on what went down tonight.

Telly frowned. The weaving tractor blocked the road in front of her. It seemed to have only a passing association with the white line in the center of the road. When it wasn't straddling the white line, the tractor hiccupped dangerously close to the edge. *Veering all over the road like a mad cow,* thought Telly. Just as well he was only doing fifteen miles an hour. She would have to overtake. She swung out around the tractor impatiently. It checked a little as she passed. She watched it in her mirror. What was he, drunk or something? Very small, anyway. Very fair. With an oddly familiar jacket. It looked for all the world like Helen Fishbone.

Blow me down, thought Telly. *Batter me from head to foot and serve me up with chips. Helen Fishbone. Answering the call.* Of all the nothing-upstairs dweebs in the neighborhood, Helen Fishbone was the most featureless and languid. A conversation with Helen Fishbone was like talking to yourself. She ran through your fingers like water, leaving nothing detectable behind. Telly'd known her for years and she was still a blank. Helen Fishbone was pallid and studious. As well as Weather Eye, she did tapestry for a hobby. Mainly tapestries of horses. That was about as close to horses as she got. Yet here she was, weaving along in the wild night in a cruddy old Foghanger tractor. She must have snuck out in the yard, past the packed and wheezing cattle. Climbed in. Started it up with a roar and a clatter. Alone. Clearly, there was a lot more to Helen Fishbone than a bit of needlepoint and a bad haircut.

Telly flipped on full headlights again. The road ahead was a little more demanding than she'd bargained for. The Cape Edge turn should be just about—just about *here*, she thought, jamming down to second. As Telly plunged right on the sea-smelling turn between the hedges she thought she saw the tractor winking an indicator. Good for Helen Fishbone. At least there was *one* other person on the right track. Getting a meeting on the strength of a bulletin message as wild as the one she'd posted was a long shot, Telly knew. But that was part of the test. Anyone who wasn't prepared to show up somewhere rude and lonely at two o'clock in the morning in the middle of a howling storm was better left in bed. Only the boldest, the most committed, would make it. Helen Fishbone was *one* she could count on. How many others had the courage?

One or two more than she'd thought, in the event. The concrete shelter in the Cape Edge parking lot housed a many-limbed monster with several heads. Flickering flashlights divided the monster into six or seven separate ghouls as she slammed shut the car and crunched across to meet them. Had she put on the handbrake? She went back to check, heaving it on some more. Then she took a deep breath. What would she say? She would keep it simple. It was simple. They wouldn't know she was Weather Eye. They wouldn't know anything except her message and the pricking of their thumbs. They all felt the world out of kilter. They felt it when the wind blew at night. They felt it badly enough to bring them to the Edge. Now it was up to Weather Eye to take them one step beyond.

She was more than equal to it. Hadn't she died and

come back? Driven home alone, when she couldn't drive more'n a fish could? Calmly, Telly approached the shelter lit by flashlights and its many-headed monster. She wasn't about to let a bunch of scabby boys unnerve her now. She was just about sick of —

"Hoozat?" A beam flashed her up and down. "Know who that is, Crips?"

Another flashlight, blinding her this time. Telly shielded her face.

"Teresa-wheeza windfarm, isn't it?" The beam dropped and pooled in the shelter. "'S only Telly Craven," said Simon Elliot flatly. "Yo, Crips. What time's it now?"

Crips shined his flashlight on his wrist. "Five to two, just on. Where's them Mars bars? You left 'em at home, you die."

Terry Crippen, thought Telly, amazed. She wouldn't have pegged Crips for a Weather Eye. Terry Crippen was an animal who wore clothes and happened to look like a person. Probably Simon Elliot had brought him with him. As well as Crips and Si, there were two or three other boys she didn't know. Bobbing anxiously in the background, half a head taller than anyone else, she recognized that long streak of snot Hugh Pridham. He only lived up the road. She supposed that was why he'd come. She couldn't imagine he'd bother, otherwise. He wasn't the most dynamic person you ever met. Six boys. Weren't there any girls?

Telly nodded as she reached them. "'Lo, there. Simon. Hughie."

Simon Elliot nodded back almost imperceptibly. "You drivin' your dad's car?"

"What's it look like?"

Simon Elliot looked at the car. Then he looked at Telly. "Respect," he said, and meant it.

Crips cracked open a Mars bar. Long Hugh Pridham wiped his nose and coughed. They weren't about to make any room in the shelter for Telly. Hard men, weren't they? Front was their job. Terry Crippen was all front, with nothing much behind it except a sad appreciation of air rifles and the effect they have on small furry animals at close range. He didn't move a muscle as Telly insinuated herself beside him. They all stood awkwardly together, looking out on the wild night.

Behind the shelter and the parking lot loomed the Edge itself, a hulking wind-torn promontory forever second by a nose to Land's End, some four or five miles south, as the furthest point west in England, and the nearest—bar the Scillies—to America. Linked to the mainland by a neck of rubble, capped with a lonely tower, bounded by sickmaking drops and the smashing, crashing sea, it was second to none for spectacle. Especially tonight. Tonight the storm had whipped up an epic soundtrack to match. The boom and hiss of mighty rollers boiling in the gugs, or blowholes, deep in the cliff face made a sonorous bass beat under the battering wind. *Land's End must be taking a hammering,* thought Telly. Looking south she could just about make out the Land's End theme park and the First & Last House in England, moth-white under the last sparks of fading Fleet-Hibble. Straight ahead, an evil bank of sea mist had grown to cover the moon. The tower at the summit of Cape Edge stood out like a black paper cutout against it.

The others Telly didn't know were Sam and Gary Lightfoot. They were oddly forthcoming, for boys. Together with one David Henry from The Tinner's Arms, they'd cycled from Porth Madder, some two or three miles down the coast road. Their mountain bikes stood by the wall. They went night fishing together sometimes, explained Gary. Over beyond the point. They thought they'd come over for a laugh. David got a message on his computer. All stirred up, he was. Weird kind of night, though, wasn't it?

"This is stupid, this is," said Crips thickly, through a mouthful of chocolate. "Wha's it all about?"

"Something's weird with the weather," said Simon Elliot. "It's scary."

"Brilliant meteor shower," said David Henry. "You all Weather Eyes?"

"I am," said Simon Elliot. "Crips was over my place, so we came down together."

"I am, too," said Telly.

"Send in any temps today?" David Henry looked

superior. "I did. And two Trauma Reports. Wind and Flood, plus wind speeds."

"No," said Telly, "I forgot."

"Letting the network down," admonished David Henry, smugly. "I never missed a day since I started. Know who sent that message? I thought I'd better come in case I missed something."

"I sent the message," said Telly. "That's why we're all here."

"It's a joke, right?" David Henry looked at her. "Who made you *the* Weather Eye?"

"No one. I made myself."

"What do *you* know?"

"Things no one else does. I died and came back."

"You died. Right."

"Anyway," said Telly, "all you need to know is, the weather's upset because of—oh, because of *us*. And it's—"

"Us?" queried Sam Lightfoot.

Telly looked at him. "People. Us. The Human Race. And it's serious. That's it. Apart from what we've got to do."

"What *have* we got to do?" asked Simon Elliot earnestly.

"Something big," said Telly. "But first you have to qualify."

"Yeh, right," said Crips. "Qualify for dorks."

Telly ignored him. "We all know something's wrong, yeh? These aren't normal storms. So you turned up tonight. That's not enough. Hear that wind?" Telly lowered her voice. "There's only *us,* okay? We're the only ones listening tonight. No one else wants to hear what the wind says, because deep down everyone's afraid." She paused significantly. "This is big. You want *into* something big, you show me you've got the guts."

"Show you my backside," said Crips. "What's she talking about?"

"But what can we do?" asked Simon Elliot. "Start a leaflet campaign?"

"This is a start," said Telly. "But we can't do it if you're afraid."

"Do what?" asked David Henry.

"*New* Weather Eye. Everything's going to change."

Hughie Pridham had been quiet for a very long time indeed. Now he said: "Anyway. Your name means coward."

"What?"

"Craven," said Hughie, "means coward."

"Oh," said Telly witheringly, "you'd know."

"I'm in," said Simon Elliot. "What do I have to do?"

"Get up on the Edge." Telly folded her arms. "Up to the tower and back. And leave something in it when you get there."

"In *this* weather?" Simon Elliot turned. He looked at the awful Edge. Then he gripped his flashlight.

"Stick to the path," said Telly. Simon Elliot had sixty-three years and forty-two days left to live. Nothing would happen tonight. "Want me to hold your hand?"

That did it. They set off in a body, all except Gary Lightfoot. Telly stopped Gary Lightfoot. She couldn't see his way clear, at all. The others would be fine. About seventy-odd years apiece. But Gary Lightfoot felt different.

"Go fishing a lot?" she asked him, as they watched the flashlight beams bob up the promontory path.

"Whenever I get the chance."

"You want to be careful," said Telly.

The wind blew Gary's hair in his face. He flicked it back and hunkered down in his coat. "Think it's really our fault?"

"What?"

"The weather."

Telly thought. "Kind of."

"We're messing things up, aren't we? Wouldn't be like this if we weren't here. If people hadn't been invented."

Telly nodded. "It's getting faster."

"What is?"

"Everything. That's why something's got to happen."

There was a longish pause. "I know it's all getting messed up. But what *I* think is — " Gary held Telly's eyes, "what *I* think is, I think it'll all be all right."

Telly smiled. "That's what I think."

Gary looked at her. "Did you always wear braces?"

Telly nodded. "I have to." She paused. "Actually, I don't. It's just, everyone's wearing them."

"Why don't you stop?"

Telly looked at Gary. He had unavoidable eyes. She ran her tongue over her train tracks; train track braces she'd affected so long, everyone else had caught up with her. Braces were flavor of the month at school. If you had a sticking-out tooth, so much the better. But it wasn't essential. Lots of girls wore them when they didn't really need them. There was something about having a mouthful of metal that made them feel special, somehow. Until everyone else followed suit. It was silly, really, Telly supposed. She didn't really need hers now, she knew.

"I won't be part of it, will I?" Gary studied the Edge. "The thing that's going to happen."

Telly watched the flashlights. One was bobbing back already. The rest were over the neck dividing the Edge from the mainland. But the worst was still to come. That hanging fissure where the crags beetled down over the path and the sea smashed its brains out beneath. On a night like this the waves would practically lick their heels as they climbed it.

"Will I?" asked Gary.

"You *are* part of it," said Telly. "The Gary Lightfoot part."

The returning flashlight beam showed her Hugh Pridham loping home in overdrive with enough crashing seas in his gut to sink him for a fortnight. His nose streamed wildly as he ran. He didn't stop to wipe it.

"You're *out!*" called Telly ruthlessly. Truth was, he'd never been in. *Go home, Hughie Pridham. Go home and pull the blankets over your head.* Telly felt the rightness of it. The wind had blown out the chaff.

Telly set out as soon as she saw the victorious signal from the tower. One flash, two flashes, three — dancing in the broken-tooth windows. They made it. She would meet them halfway as she went.

"Where're you going?" shouted Gary.

Telly looked around. "Won't be long."

She met them at the neck. Crips was wild and sea-stained. The others trailed behind him, gloriously windswept, careless as Cup Final victors. Telly put her head down and passed them purposefully.

"Where you going?" screamed Crips, through the wind. "We done it. Din' you see?"

"Now me!" mouthed Telly, turning.

"Wait!" yelled Crips. "You haven't got no flashlight!"

Of course she hadn't. Why would she need one? Telly turned on her way. Each blind footfall fell in the best possible place, and the dark path helped her go. The wind lifted her on, the roaring waves warned her where the edge was, the moon showed its face obligingly at the craggy fissure where the breakers boiled below. The heather gave a spring to her step, the gorse rattled over hidden pitfalls, the tower itself buffered her from the wind blast at the summit and welcomed her in to sit down. The fusty benches inside showed her the badge the others had left there. Telly picked it up and turned it over in her hand. One of the old-style Weather Eye badges. Probably '93 or '94. When Weather Eye had started. It had been a pretty crummy logo. The badges were redesigned, now. She slipped it into her pocket and came easily down from the Edge, moving effortless-ly between and over obstacles, trusting herself, not thinking anything at all.

At last the ground cover changed. Her feet made a regular crunch. Gravel. She looked up, surprised. She was back at the shelter in the parking lot—and all at once covered in glory.

She showed them the badge. "Here. I wanted to prove I'd been up there."

"Without a flashlight," breathed Simon Elliot. "Smart."

"Mad, more like," said David Henry. "Could've killed yourself."

"No," said Telly, "I couldn't."

"Thought you were never comin' down," said Crips, uncharitably.

"He was going to go off home," said Simon Elliot. "I stopped him."

Crips looked down. Then he looked up. He met Telly's eyes with respect. "I got to hand it to you. I don't know many girls'd do that."

"I don't know many anyones," said Si. "Without a flashlight. Tough, or what?"

"I'm not tough," said Telly. It wasn't brave, when you knew there was no risk to your life. Going up without knowing if you'd ever come down again—that was brave. "I'm not tough. But you are."

They all glowed a little, even Crips. Sam Lightfoot held up his hand. "Listen. Sounds like a tractor or something."

It was. A cruddy, red Foghanger tractor, barreling down the lane, cab swaying, baler cord streaming out behind. It churned in on the gravel, cutting out abruptly. Helen Fishbone swung down.

"Sorry I'm late," she said toothily. "Is this the Weather Eye meeting? Telly? Is that you?"

Telly grinned. "What kept you?"

"I took a wrong turn somewhere up the road. Almost got to Porth Madder before I realized." She shrugged self-deprecatingly. "Hopeless sense of direction."

"You did really well getting here at all."

"Hope I haven't missed much. Denny was going to come, but then he got scared. So I came all by myself. What are we doing?"

"You got to go up the Edge," said Crips maliciously. "Up the tower an' back in the dark."

"That's right," chimed Simon Elliot. "Show you got the guts."

Helen Fishbone looked at the Edge. Then she looked at Telly.

"Ignore them." Telly smiled. "You're brave enough already."

Telly weighed them up. There were only three Weather Eyes among them—Simon Elliot, David Henry, and Helen Fishbone. Counting herself as *the* Eye, four Weather Eyes. Four Weather Eyes, plus two fishermen (the Lightfoots) and a deadhead (no prize).

They watched her expectantly. The first light of dawn reached up behind the sea. At last Telly smiled.

"Something's going to happen, isn't it?" whispered Helen Fishbone. "That's what the message said."

The early dawning sun flooded Telly's face. Another bright new day. "Yes," she nodded softly. "Something's going to happen."

Sam Lightfoot leaned against his brother, Gary. He'd hardly said a word all night. But he'd thought plenty. David Henry thoughtfully picked his nails. Crips sat back on his hands. Helen Fishbone watched the lightening sky. They all began to wonder what would happen, and the wondering was different for each of them. Telly searched their faces. They were as ready as they'd ever be.

"Listen up. Here's the plan," she said.

6

K E E P I N G   O U T

T H E   D R A F T S

"What's Uncle Race like?" asked Race, trailing Dad out to the pickup.

"Race Peters?" Pat Craven grimaced. "Don't ask. Like a monkey in a fruit shop. Worse."

The borrowed pickup was covered in sand. It had rained in the night—big, ugly drops of dirty sand, scoured up by the wind from some desperate desert half a hemisphere distant. Pat Craven threw his waterproof jacket onto the front seat. Then he dragged it out again and checked that his wallet was in it. Fine. He'd primed Mrs. Ruddock. What else? The turbines should turn over nicely until he got back. Strange kind of lull in the weather. It didn't feel right, somehow. He checked his watch. Eleven o'clock already. Something told Pat Craven he'd better go, if he was going. The sooner he went, the sooner he'd be back. He needed to have a chat with his supplier about a replacement blade for that turbine. Hopefully, he wouldn't need to replace the spinner as well. They might well have a blade in stock. Arrangements would have to be made. A truck hired. He wouldn't be more than a few hours, at the most. Straight up the A38 to Heyderstrom Technics, back early evening at the latest. What, after all, could happen?

"Why can't we go to Australia and see him?" asked Race. Ever since he'd dug out the photo of his uncle and looked at it—*before* he'd dug out the photo of his uncle and looked at it—Race had had a feeling. A feeling as familiar as the well-tugged lock of hair he coiled around his finger in moments of concentration; a feeling about an uncle he didn't even *know*. It wasn't fair. Why couldn't he even know him? "Why can't we?" persisted Race.

"Why can't we what?" Pat Craven slapped his chest pocket for his checkbook.

"See Uncle Race Peters. Why don't we ever see him?"

"Funny, your mother was saying the very same thing last week. Seen my map? The one with the blue cover?"

"'S in the glove compartment of our car."

"It would be," grumbled Pat Craven. "Blessed nuisance having to borrow Will Fishbone's honky pickup. Probably blow up before I get there."

Race half turned to look at Telly. Telly stood waiting by the gate. She felt too guilty about the car to see Dad off any closer. Telly gave Race The Look. The Look that said: "Tell and You Die."

Pat Craven winked. "Hey. Cheer up. Only joking. I'll be back before you know it. Mrs. Ruddock's coming in to keep an eye on things. I think it's meat pies for lunch."

Race brightened. "I like Mrs. Ruddock's meat pies, I do."

Pat Craven swung in behind the wheel. He raised his voice to Telly. "Back around six or seven. Stay in the house if the wind gets up. See you later. Be good."

"'Bye, Dad," waved Telly, bleakly.

She watched the pickup roar off up the lane. Being able to get around in the car was an essential part of being Weather Eye, but the price she was paying to keep it was getting steeper by the moment. Race didn't help. Race had thought of something.

He passed her coldly at the gate. "If you don't find Dewie this afternoon, I'm going to tell Dad about the car soon as he gets back, so you better get him."

Telly watched her brother up the path. Not bad. He was growing up already.

"You'll catch it, too," she shouted, as an afterthought.

Race went inside without looking back. Telly was strange today. Strange yesterday. Especially yesterday morning. At breakfast she'd been bright and crisp and bossy, the way she was when she bought up Park

Avenue in Monopoly, only more so. Shiny face. Straggly, sea-smelling hair. Offered to undo the knot in the laces of his sneakers. No reaction at all when he pinched the top of the milk for his cereal. Definitely strange. Race had an idea why. He'd more than half an idea she'd been out somewhere in the night.

The reason he knew was simple. He'd snuck into Telly's room, frightened, around two o'clock in the morning, when the storm had woken him up. But the bed had been cold and strange and Telly hadn't been in it. Darkness downstairs. Snoring from Dad's room. He'd felt her bed. It wasn't even warm. The quilt registered a Telly shape, where she'd lain down some time ago on top of it; but she hadn't been in bed and under it. If she wasn't in bed in her room—and she wasn't with Dad downstairs—where *was* she? Race had crept back to his own bed and lain awake, more wondering than frightened, until Telly and the wind and cold empty beds had made a strange mixed-up dream in his head that took him away until morning.

That had been the night before last. All yesterday he'd been helping Dad, and he hadn't seen much of Telly. He and Dad had spent the afternoon way up in the shuddering cabin at the top of the damaged turbine. With trembling legs and a safety harness that shackled him to the ladder (Race had pleaded—how could he fall?) Race had led the white-knuckle climb inside the tower. It was way too exciting to worry about wobbly legs or the cold draft funneling up from the bottom; he wasn't often allowed to the top of the towers.

Squeezing between the main bearing and the cabin wall, Dad had accessed the spinner from the inside, assessing damage, feeding back cover plates to Race. Race had passed him tools in return. There wasn't much room in the cabin. The machine bed, with its steel-sheathed moving parts, took up almost all the room there was. Above the hatch in the roof the windvane buzzed; at Race's feet the mighty yaw gear, controlling cabin direction, intruded through the floor. Race could recognize the gearbox and the generator, but he was pretty woolly about the rest of the machinery. He was only glad it wasn't in action. He kept a respectful distance from the generator, all the same. What do you give a sick turbine? Answer: lots of room.

At last Dad had sat back and grunted. "Major works. Have to get a crane in." They greased the gearbox anyway. That was one job they wouldn't have to do again for a while, said Dad. Climbing down, they'd checked the twin microcomputers in the base of the tower. Every turbine tower had its computers monitoring wind speed and power output. Pat Craven called up the week's log. The graph showed winds peaking at hurricane force twelve in the early hours of Monday, eighteenth October—

around about the time of Telly's accident, pointed out Dad. The turbine blade had shattered when the wind had hit it at a hundred and twelve miles an hour.

That was yesterday. This was today. The meat pies at lunchtime were lush—a culiminary delight, opined Race, stuffing down an extra half on top of the one he'd eaten. "Culinary delight," corrected Telly. Mrs. Ruddock smiled a lot and watched him. After lunch Telly announced she was off to Helen Fishbone's.

Race looked at her significantly. "Hope Dad gets the car back soon," he said. "Don't you?" Telly slammed out abruptly. Race grinned. His confidence in Telly knew no bounds. He looked forward to finding Dewie at home before teatime.

Mrs. Ruddock settled over the paper in the living room after the washing up, spilling her glasses and her sewing bits willy nilly off the arms of the armchair as she settled herself into it. Race picked everything up. Then he told Mrs. Ruddock earnestly and at length about baby pandas in China, and how there wouldn't be any more unless everyone stopped building cities an' stuff because of them eating bamboo. "What?" said Mrs. Ruddock, feeling she'd missed something, somewhere. Race rubbed his head. He felt heavy and hot, as though he could hardly breathe.

Mrs. Ruddock looked at him over her glasses. "Open a window, Race, would you? It's close this afternoon."

After a while, Mrs. Ruddock dozed off. Race

nipped into the kitchen. Getting out a tea bag, flour, and coffee grounds, he whipped up a quick diarrhea special for the step. Mrs. Ruddock was untried soil. He pictured her face when she stepped in it. He considered opening a can of Vegetable Wholesoup on the floor and telling her he'd been sick, but there weren't enough carrots in the picture on the front of the can. You had to have bits of carrot for sick.

After he'd embellished the step, Race came wearily in. Everything was heavy. Everything was tired. He sighed and settled down on the floor, drawing a picture of a flaming comet, coloring it in so violently that he met the carpet underneath. Mrs. Ruddock slept on. The paper slipped from the arm of her chair. DAY THREE OF HURRICANE HELL screamed the headline. WORSE TO COME SAYS WEATHER CENTER. Race considered Mrs. Ruddock's sleeping face. Then he considered her sewing. She'd been cutting out something on her lap. An oval-shaped something in paper, pinned to a square of pathetic, floral-pattern fabric. Race had never been able to resist a pair of scissors. He loved making things. He loved helping other people make things. He would help Mrs. Ruddock make her thingie.

With infinite care, Race picked up the scissors in Mrs. Ruddock's lap. It wasn't going to be easy with her sleeping hand across part of the fabric. He would have to work around it. Digging in, he made the best of his way along the line she'd started cutting. *Stick to lines*, he advised the *Make It With Race* audience. *That way you can't go wrong.* He plowed on, making a turn with extreme difficulty through ninety degrees without introducing his elbow into Mrs. Ruddock's face. Tongue out, the way it always was when he was concentrating, Race severed the shape and lifted it. *Take pins out,* he told his audience. *Make sure it doesn't—*

Race looked with horror at the large, oval-shaped hole in the lap of Mrs. Ruddock's dress. The rolled-up tops of her stockings were plainly visible through its interestingly jagged edges. Suddenly Race felt like going somewhere else altogether.

Upstairs the air felt funny. Something was missing—something you only noticed when it wasn't there anymore. Race opened Telly's bedroom window and looked out. Incredibly, the turbines had ground to a halt. He'd missed their regular swishing, their cartwheeling arms in the sky. And any hint of a wind. Race looked up. The sky seemed a lot lower than usual, like a ceiling you could touch if you wanted. Nothing moved under that ceiling. Nothing wanted to. The lull was almost as unnerving, in its way, as the storm. Like an eye, thought Race. Like when it's an eye in the middle of a hurricane, then the other side hits you after. Maybe that's just what it was. That hammer-heavy ceiling was pressing the life out of everything. There was no escape. Nothing had the energy to drag itself away. Race sat spellbound by the window. A thought came to him so big and so clear it seemed to have thought itself.

Something was going to happen. Something big. It was happening already. It had been simmering a long while. Now it was coming to the boil. All at once, Race felt frightened. When would Telly be back? She'd slammed out and never said a time. Dad wouldn't be home for ages after he'd said he would, Race knew from bitter experience. Race had spent long hours at Heyderstrom Technics listening to Dad and Mr. Hansen talking pitch-regulated upwind rotors and time delays for yaw connections. He'd practically had to prop his eyes open.

Race moved away from the window. He looked around. Then he sat down at Telly's desk. The computer stared blankly back. Race flipped it on. As options built slowly onscreen, Race began to feel better. Here, staring him in the face, was the chance he'd been waiting for. It was a good thing Telly'd gone out. At last he could try out her password. It had taken Race a week or two to get the last couple of letters, passing casually behind Telly just as she was logging in. You couldn't guess the end of it, because it was a word that didn't make sense. Race optioned GLOBE.QUEST., the way Telly always did. Then he keyed in LODESTAR. He had no idea why. It was just what Telly did. Then things got a bit difficult. It was at this stage that Telly always sent him away if he was anywhere near the screen. Internet Yes or No? asked the screen. Race took a chance and pressed *Y* on the keyboard. Immediately the familiar Weather Eye Symbol occupied a box on the screen. Race optioned the box with growing excitement. He flipped on Telly's desk light. Getting dark already. It was only four o'clock.

A list of options winked up against a blue and green map of the world. Weather Eye Internet. Global Exchange. Bulletin Board. Weather Center Updates. Eye Log & Records. Using the mouse, Race clicked on Global Exchange. The screen beeped nastily. Nothing global happened at all. Race centered his screen arrow and clicked on Eye Log & Records, but the beep tripped him up again. He moused all the options in turn, reaping a series of beeps that were beginning to upset him. Then he noticed: "Your Weather Eye password, please" in blue at the bottom of the screen. Race swallowed. Time for the magic word he'd gleaned from Telly. Holding his breath, he keyed in NOSTRADAMUS carefully. Nothing happened. Then he hit RETURN. "Hi, Telly! Screen Options Viable," offered the screen, chattily. Race grinned. He was in. The world of Weather Eye was his to explore. Where would he go first? How about Bulletin Board? Bulletin Board would have bulletins. Whatever they were. Unhurriedly optioning B.B., Race settled down to enjoy himself. Then he heard voices outside.

Race bobbed up at the window. Then he bobbed

down again, thinking furiously. Simon Elliot. And Greville Jackett. Simon Elliot and Greville Jackett, halfway up the path already. Why? He would have to find out before they reached the front door and stirred up Mrs. Ruddock. Of course, she would have to wake up sometime and notice the hole in her dress. But maybe he could think of something first. Something like running off to London and never coming back.

Race opened the window and leaned out. Simon and Greville looked up. "Telly there?" asked Si.

"She went out," Race said shortly. "You better go home. Something's going to happen."

"Low atmospheric pressure," nodded Simon. "Noticed it this morning. Where'd she go?"

"Round Helen Fishbone's. Won't be back for ages." Race rubbed his head. Even speaking was an effort in the syrupy air. How dark it was. How threatening.

"Tell 'er Grev's in, will you?" said Simon Elliot importantly.

"In what?"

"*In*. She'll know. The big one."

"The big one," echoed Race blankly.

Greville Jackett stirred. "Better get going," he told Si. "See that cloud?"

They looked up. It wasn't really a cloud. It was more like a lowering of the ceiling. Soon there would be no room under it to breathe.

"Did you see a rabbit down the village?" asked Race, with an effort. "I lost mine day before yesterday."

"What color?" asked Si.

"Like, gray with brown and white bits."

"If he got up the main road you won't see him no more," said Greville Jackett. "Why did the rabbit cross the road?"

"To show he had guts?" Simon Elliot smirked.

"He won't get run over or anything," said Race earnestly. "He's too clever. But he might've gone to live with someone else."

"Yeah, right." Greville Jackett checked the sky. "Anyway. I'm out of here."

"Don't forget or Crips'll get you," called Simon, backing away down the path.

"What?"

"Grev!" shouted Si, his voice falling flat on the air. "Tell Telly Grev's in!"

Grev's in. Race gave them a thumbs up and watched them out of sight. Grev's *in*. Telly—Simon Elliot came round with that nut, Greville Jackett, and he's *in*. In what?

Race felt the shock on his face when the rainstorm burst outside, torrenting down like someone upstairs optioned DELUGE. It made a sound like a million scampering feet on the roof. Nasty little feet. The rain drummed faster and harder. All the little feet stamped together. Race shivered. He looked behind him. Then he got up and closed the door, jamming it underneath with a sweater against Drafts. It was surprising how small a gap they could get in.

As soon as he turned, the Bulletin Board caught his eye. Open-mouthed, Race sat down at the computer. The messages flooded the screen, one tripping another like a landslide:

```
Ouch! Big trouble in little China. Mother of
'quakes, Richter scale 6.4, hits downtown LA
yesterday noon. Many aftershocks, my father's
restaurant is a total no-go area. Bridges and
freeways are mucho collapso—Uncle Chin (in
construction) rubs his hands. Not so funny:
hospital requests blood. My parents will give
for sure. Wei Chin, Chinatown, Los Angeles.
```

▼

```
Mes amies—we are receiving 54 millimeters of
rain in Monte Carlo today! We are having average
yearly rainfall a thousand millimeters. So that
we are receiving over five percent in a day! We
are all sandbags, my grandmother is flooding
her house and moving in with us. I meet my
friends. My friends say, What is Weather Eye? I
tell them no fear. Elena Delarge, Monaco.
```

▼

```
The Mississippi—river or ocean? Identity
crisis, or what? The river keeps swelling
like a cane toad. Poplar Bluff, Dyersburg,
```

Blytheville, Henderson—all washed up. Friday we finally moved out of temporary accommodation (a rank hut in Snoozeville, upstate Missouri) and on up to St. Louis, neat! Biggest flood since Noah took up home improvement over western Kentucky. Rain forever. Pass the rubber duck. Freeman Fischer, Illinois, US.

▼

I am having a big trouble with my schoolwork, any wonder? We are flood-damage, over thirty kilometers, many cows feet-up, school is kaput. I am wondering how it globals? Weather Eye Sensi, Nederland.

▼

Help, you guys, no videos since typhoon Erma hit Auckland! Waipoona Beach Video wiped out—please send any you can, Bruce Lee or Die Hard, urgent c/o Logan Bush College, Mnt. Wellington, New Zealand. Please address to me, Pago Atata, not teacher. My teacher runs around like a crazy man.

Race rubbed his eyes. On it went, and on. Ramon Sepulveda, Tampico, Mexico, complaining a storm surge wrecked his father's boat; Cassie Nolan from Brisbane, Australia, whining about the Brickfielder, a hot dry wind from the desert, bringing bush fires this year like you never saw in your life, not if you lived to a hundred. There was even a message from

Calcutta: Imrah Jamshedpur, reporting winds of more than a hundred and sixty kilometers an hour in the Bay of Bengal.

Earthquakes, floods, typhoons. In America, Holland, Monaco—wherever that was—New Zealand, India, Bay of Bengal. So many kids crying panic. And those were the ones with computers. How many others lay shivering under the quilt when the wind blew at night? If they had quilts— or beds, or houses, left? Race swallowed. What he'd long suspected was true. The weather had gone mad. No wonder Telly'd been tight-lipped. It was worse, *much* worse, than he'd thought.

Suddenly the computer went down, blanking out abruptly in the moment the light went off. The wind hit the house like a wall. Race stared stupidly at the screen. Then he jumped up, his heart pounding. He made sure the window was secure. The darkness outside was complete. It was pretty dark inside, as well. Fumbling Telly's little reading flashlight from underneath her pillow, Race turned. The sweater under the bedroom door was moving. Race watched with horror. The sweater was actually lifting as the wind forced its way through and over the house with the kind of power that could drive a straw into a tree trunk. Race knew, with leaden certainty, that the Drafts would get him this time. This was the chance they'd been waiting for. But they wouldn't get in without a struggle.

After he'd made his lonely patrol through the bedrooms, blocking every window, every Drafthole he could with whatever he could lay his hands on, Race went heavily downstairs. He paid particular attention to the front door, locking it securely and forcing towels in the gaps around it with a ruler. It took Race ten minutes' effort and four blue hand towels to make the front door Draft-proof. He wandered into the darkened living room, every nerve on edge. The sight of Mrs. Ruddock brought him up sharp. How could she sleep through this? What was she, deaf? Yes. That was just what she was. Skirting the open-mouthed and gently snoring Mrs. Ruddock, Race set to work on the living room windows. Not a moment too soon. The curtains were active already as an icy Draft outside fingered the inefficient seal between stonework and window frame. Race knew how to deal with window Drafts. He fetched Dad's big roll of masking tape.

In an orgy of ripping noises Race made the windows secure, running a line of sticky tape all around each frame. Mrs. Ruddock stirred in her chair. Race held his breath. She didn't wake up. But she was definitely surfacing slowly, like a polar submarine after months beneath the icecap. Nothing could stop her surfacing. She would presently pop up, hatches open, torpedoes armed, to give him a broadside about the hole in the front of her dress. Nothing could be more certain—or more entirely bearable in the face of the threat outside. Race ducked out to the kitchen. He'd rather face a zillion Mrs. Ruddocks than let in a single Draft. He'd almost rather wake her than fight the fight alone. Almost, but not quite.

The phone by the kitchen door was dead, as well as the kitchen lights. Race replaced the receiver with a hollow sound. He'd never felt more alone. Telly's voice—or even Helen Fishbone's—might have made a difference. Telly wouldn't come home in this. She would hunker down where she was. Race let his thoughts wander over the tempestuous fields outside, to the place—warm and dry, he hoped—where a large fluffy rabbit, gray with brown and white bits, was somewhere, somehow, weathering the storm. Race hoped poor Dewie wasn't as frightened as he was.

After he'd taped the kitchen windows and jammed the sill with tea towels, Race had a sudden thought. Wasn't—wasn't the window in the back bedroom usually open? The old back bedroom, upstairs? Dropping everything except his flashlight, Race pounded up to the landing. He listened. A thundering boom from the oldest part of the house— just when you thought it was safe to sit in the kitchen. How could he have forgotten the old back bedroom? The Drafts were having a party in the very room he'd slept in when he was small enough not to annoy them.

Race listened in the corridor. The party was wild

and barely contained by the door. Now they were in, they were letting rip. He could hear them blundering around the furniture. Booming in the chimney. Roaring around the walls in a horrible dance of possession, owl eyes gleeful in the dark. There was only one thing to do. But Race didn't run off. Instead, he opened the door and went in.

Sobbing with terror, Race bolted across the room and closed the open window. Then he ran for his life down the stairs, headlong into the kitchen. He sobbed all the time he was searching for the candles in the drawer; all the time he was searching for the matches; all the time he was lighting the candle. In the light of the single white candle stuck to a saucer, Race sat down. He didn't want to remember the way the streaming curtains in the back bedroom had met his face before he'd reached the open window; the horrible way they'd stroked him when he'd closed it.

Race was making channels with a matchstick in the hot candlewax pooling in the saucer when the back door gave a little. Calmer now, absorbed in a miniature wax landscape he alone could engineer, Race didn't really notice. When he did, it was too late. The back door gave a little more. Something was coming in. Terror jumped up like a giant. Race felt his legs turn to water.

"Race!" Mrs. Ruddock's voice, from the living room. "Race! Put the light on, will you, dear, I had an awful dream!"

Race watched the back door opening, speech-lessly. He couldn't have answered Mrs. Ruddock if his life had depended on it. It couldn't be Telly, in this weather. It couldn't be Dad—too early. It couldn't be Mum—away for another week. It could only be the big one. The biggest Draft of all.

"Dad?" croaked Race, hopefully. "Telly?"

The door opened, finally. The stuff he'd jammed around it had almost kept him safe. But in the end, the only defense was—

It was a very tall Draft, the one they'd sent to get him. Boxy shoulders, shiny, wet-looking limbs, webbed with something long and vague as its body. Race looked with dread for its owlish head, clutch-ing his candle in the certain teeth of despair.

The tall Draft flung itself in in a blast of leaf litter. It set down a suitcase. It looked at its feet.

"Looks like I stepped in something," it said in an oddly cracked twang. "Sorry about that. Pile of dog-doo the size of Queensland on the step."

Race had heard a twang like that before. On *Neighbours*. And *Sheep Station 702*, the latest Aussie soap. Queensland, he thought. Australia. No Draft would come all the way from Australia, just to terri-fy *him*. He had it all wrong. It had to be someone they knew who'd just come . . . someone Australian they . . . it had to be . . .

"Race!" called Mrs. Ruddock. "Who's that com-ing in the back?"

"Uncle Race?" whispered Race.

Uncle Race Peters shrugged off his long, wet Australian raincoat, bowled his Australian hat into a chair, and turned to greet his namesake with the sunniest of Australian smiles and an outstretched hand like a plate.

"Mag's boy, wouldn't it be? Put it there," he said.

7

T H E   C A L M I N G

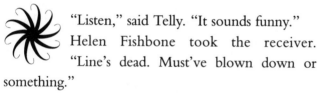 "Listen," said Telly. "It sounds funny."

Helen Fishbone took the receiver. "Line's dead. Must've blown down or something."

"I better get back," said Telly.

"Stay over," said Helen, replacing the phone. "You can't go home in this."

"Tell Telly she'd better stay over!" shouted Helen Fishbone's mother. "She can't go home in this!"

Helen grinned. She flashed her flashlight up the hall. "Come upstairs. You said we'd start at seven. It's almost seven now."

"Hear that?" shouted Mrs. Fishbone, over the tinny transistor in the kitchen. "It says giant waves and a high tide sent tons of water crashing over the seawall at Dagmouth. Winds up to ninety miles an hour. Cod or scrod?"

Helen Fishbone grimaced. "What?" she shouted back.

"Cod or scrod?" repeated Mrs. Fishbone. "Tell Telly she can have either. Ask Denny what he wants. Thank heavens for Calor gas. At least I can still cook."

The back door erupted. Will Fishbone burst into the kitchen, his waterproofs running a river, his sodden hat molded to his scalp. He swung a smoke-stained oil lamp onto the table.

"Can't do no more for 'em now," he said, with an air of finality. "All the ewes is in the barn. Charles backed the tractor up against the door. That should hold it. I never seen Hoar Top mast go down in twenty years, but he's down tonight. God knows how Pat Craven'll get back tonight in the pickup, I—"

"Cod or scrod?" interrupted Mrs. Fishbone loudly. "It's giant waves at Dagmouth. Lifeboat's on standby up Porth Madder. It says they lost count of the yachts that've slipped their moorings."

"Never seen it worse." Helen Fishbone's father sat down heavily at the table. "I tell you, the weather's gone mad. Cod."

Telly followed Helen's flashlight reluctantly up to her bedroom, wishing it were her own. Truth was, she felt pretty awful. Two hours with Helen Fishbone was more than enough for anyone. She'd wanted to see what made the Fishbone tick, following the outstanding turnout with the tractor. But there was nothing to find out. Helen Fishbone's mind was as vacant as Dewie's. Dewie. Telly felt exhausted, remembering her search. The air had been so dead-weight heavy, searching the fields for Dewie, she'd practically had to drag herself to Foghanger. All in all, it had been a puddingy, do-nothing kind of afternoon. Now the wind was up—raging at the windows, boxing the trees outside like the last two days had been a practice bout. When would it ever stop? The feeling that something was about to happen sat more heavily than ever on Telly. It was making her ill. So was the Fishbone's bedroom.

Helen Fishbone's bedroom was a shrine to Scott Lucas, star of *Echo Beach*. Scott Lucas looked down from every wall in every conceivable position, his denim-blue eyes smouldering under fiercely engineered hair. Telly sat down uncomfortably. Embarrassing, or what? *Echo Beach* was history. Even when *Echo Beach* had been hot, Scott Lucas had always been the one that nobody fancied. The only reason anyone ever watched it in the first place was Randy Coverdale, the surfer with the puppy-dog eyes. Helen Fishbone was a seriously sad person. Liking Scott Lucas was something to keep to yourself. Saddest of all, she didn't know it.

"I thought you liked Craig Engels now," said Telly.

"He's all right." Helen centered her flashlight on her desk.

Telly waited, but that was it. The wind blasted the window. Helen sighed. "When's it ever going to stop?"

"Climate's changing," said Telly. "More storms, more wind, more everything."

"My mum says there was this *huge* storm when I was little. Fifteenth October 1987. Three days before my birthday. Know how many trees blew down?"

"A million?" hazarded Telly.

"*Nineteen* million. My mum reckons it all started round about then. Round about '87."

"Probably right," said Telly. "It's always been stormy for us."

"Not like this," said Helen, watching the window.

"No," said Telly softly, "not like this."

"What's going on?"

Telly shrugged. "A change. I don't know."

"What can we do?"

"Be ready."

Rain battered the window. Helen Fishbone jumped up and moved her collection of china animals away from the leak in the sill. She looked out. All that separated her from the wildest night on record was a double layer of glass. Helen Fishbone had been frightened by the weather for a long time. She wanted to do something about it. Telly Craven, the Telly Craven she'd known for years, seemed to know what to do. It was exciting. The mysterious message on the computer bulletin board had been exciting. So exciting, she'd jumped in the tractor and driven out alone in the middle of the night! She hardly recognized herself. And this was only the beginning.

"So what *is* the plan?" asked Helen.

"I told you before. It's all down to us."

"I know what you told us," said Helen. "We stop whatever we're doing at seven o'clock, exactly. But what does the tree mean?"

"The tree," said Telly carefully, "is what we think about."

"Because the next meeting's at the Wizzen Tree, right?" Helen Fishbone pointed to the computer printout on her bedroom wall. "That's what the second message says."

The printout on the wall looked pretty good. This time the message was a picture. A tree in a meadow, stretching its arms in delight. It had gone out the previous morning. Telly'd built the electric-blue tree carefully in the Paintbox program, pulling in a wide green foreground. Then she'd saved it into a file she could post direct to the bulletin board. She'd made sure Weather Eyes everywhere had a good, long look at the Tree in the Meadow by optioning PRIVILEGED OVERWRITE. It made an arresting image. The caption looked pretty good, too:

STATUS CODE KAOS

PRIVILEGED OVERWRITE

SEVEN O'CLOCK CALMING

Weather Eyes International! Blown away by the weather? The Tree in the Meadow wants YOU. Save and print this picture and pin it on your wall. Think about it. Seven o'clock, your time, EVERY NIGHT. One Safe Haven in Our Minds. YOUR WEATHER EYE.

Network Southwest: The Wizzen Tree, Bready Lookout, Friday at midnight. Message ends.

"We're thinking about the Wizzen Tree, right?" repeated the Fishbone.

"The tree's important." Telly looked up.

"The tree at Bready Lookout?"

"No," said Telly, "the Tree in the Meadow. The meadow where everything's still."

Helen Fishbone looked at Telly. Was Telly all right since her accident? That awful night three days ago, when the storm had struck like a fist? The night Helen's fourteen-year-old brother, Denny, had comforted her with a paperback entitled *Nostradamus, His Prophecies,* explaining how old Nostradamus reckoned the world would end in 1999 so she might as well give him the money she was going to spend on his present now—they probably wouldn't see Christmas. Wouldn't need her camera, would she? Or her new watch. Not if the world was going to end. She might as well hand them over. It would make him happy for the short while he had left. It wasn't much to ask.

"That's only part of it, right?" Helen Fishbone searched Telly's eyes. "Then we send out messages and have meetings and save everyone from the weather, right?"

"Right," said Telly coldly. "We're going to save the world."

"But how?" Helen Fishbone wilted. "We're just a bunch of kids."

Telly watched her realize. "We're Weather Eyes. We watch the weather. We send in temperatures and wind speeds."

The Fishbone digested this. "Why did you ask the others to choose people, and not me?"

"Choose people?"

"For the next meeting. Why didn't you ask me?"

"They're boys," said Telly. "They have to have something to do."

"Three minutes to seven." Helen checked her watch. "So we're all kind of, sitting together —"

"Calmly."

"We're all sitting calmly, thinking about the same thing at the same time. Then what? What will it do?"

"Bring us together," said Telly, tiring of questions.

"We're together on the network."

"This is different. All they ever talk about on the

network are floods and gales and storm damage. This is something safe. Something good, for a change."

"A picture of a tree." *Sounds a bit silly,* thought Helen. "The Tree in the Meadow, right?"

"Right," said Telly. But she didn't feel right. She felt just about as bad as you'd ever want to feel at a friend's house. It wasn't the battering wind at the window. It wasn't the smell of frying cod downstairs. It wasn't even Scott Lucas. It was a certainty pooling inside her, heavy as molten lead. Something was going to happen. It was happening already. There was nothing she could do. Saliva welled up in Telly's mouth. It felt like . . . felt like . . . Drowning.

Denny put his head around the door.

"Bog off," said Helen flatly.

Denny smirked. "Having a meeting, are we?"

"We were," said Telly. "Weather Eye."

"Weather Eye's rubbish." Denny came in. Putting his hands in his pockets, he considered the storm outside. "Weather's getting worse. Probably blow us away. Not much point worrying about it. Nothing anyone can do."

Helen watched him. "Make it worse, why don't you?"

"This book I've got says the world's going to end before Christmas," said Denny cheerfully. "Might as well do what we want."

"Did you want something?" Helen asked acidly.

"All I want's a decent watch—" he eyed Telly's "—or a bit of cash. A bit of cash'd be nice."

Telly cleared her throat. "Make you happy, would it?"

Denny shrugged. "Can't take it with you, can you? Might as well let someone else enjoy it. Not much point hanging on to cash. Not if the world's going to end."

"What if he's right?" whispered Helen.

"He isn't. Why can't you leave us alone?"

"I could for a couple of quid," said Denny brazenly.

"He's only doing it 'cos it's almost seven," said Helen. "I *told* him not to come in at seven o'clock."

"Haven't you got something better to do?" Telly rose. A wave of nausea hit her. If she was going to throw up, she'd make sure she did it over Denny. "We're only wasting time."

"I got all the time in the world, me." Denny lounged back against the wall. "What's left of it, that is."

Telly looked at Denny. Denny was frightening Helen. He'd gone and put his great fat foot in the mood she'd conjured so carefully. Enough was enough. Telly held the door. "Get out."

"Nice friends you got," Denny told his sister. "She always like this?"

"Get out *now* or—"

"Or what?"

"Or I'll tell you the day you're going to die." Telly

paused, for effect. "The year, the month, the week—the *exact* day—and then you'll have to live the rest of your life knowing."

"Don't be stupid," said Denny, uncomfortably. "Don't say things like that."

"Ivan the Terrible wanted to know what day he'd die, so he got these three wise women to tell him," lectured Telly. "Know what happened? He got so scared he fell down in a fit and died the day before they'd told him he would. I can tell you the year, if you like," she went on conversationally, "or just the day and the month. The date's not a million miles from—"

Denny straightened. "This is sick. I got things to do."

"The date's not a million miles from the fifteenth of—"

"Jinx!" Denny jammed his fingers in his ears. "Jinx on you not me, jinx on you not me, jinx on . . ." Chanting loudly, he walked out. ". . . you not me, jinx on you not me, jinx on . . ." They heard him chanting childishly all the way up the corridor until a door slammed.

"Nice one." Helen grinned. "He's always saying *I'm* stupid being scared of nothing. He's pretty stupid himself."

"Stupid and wrong," breathed Telly, leaning against the door. Not enough air. Rising waters—somewhere.

"All that stuff about the end of the world. There's nothing to be afraid of—is there?" whispered Helen.

Telly swallowed. "Nothing except part two."

"Part two of what?"

"Part two of the plan."

"What's part two of the plan?" whispered Helen Fishbone intensely.

"Wait till Friday." The neck of Telly's sweater suddenly felt too tight. Dark waters. No one to help. A terrible struggle, alone. "Friday night, at the Lookout. I'll pick you up, if you like."

"Seven o'clock, exactly," said the Fishbone, over her watch.

At the stroke of seven they sat together quietly. Helen Fishbone sat quietly counting the dark brown cross-stitches on the tapestry she'd recently finished. The knight on his richly caparisoned charger, on the wall between Telly's tree picture and a particularly winsome Scott Lucas, had taken the Fishbone a very long time indeed to complete. Tapestry was comforting. It took her mind off the weather. Seven o'clock Calming missed her by a mile. Telly was strange. Too strange to argue with. Still, it was exciting.

Telly sat quietly, being with Weather Eyes everywhere, doing the same thing at the same time. Those who'd got the message. Weather Eyes everywhere in the same time zone would be thinking about the Tree in the Meadow. Soon seven o'clock would come to Canada, Russia, Japan—and *they* would be thinking about it. That was the beauty of it. As the earth turned and seven o'clock in the evening came around for everyone, someone, somewhere, would be Calming at any given moment. That way the world would be covered. Everyone would be part of it. Everyone would feel better.

Closing her eyes, Telly summoned up the Tree. She remembered her journey as though it were yesterday. Through the tunnel. Into the light. Across the meadow, softly. Calm, thought Telly. And still. One safe haven in our minds. The strange phrase repeated itself, over and over and over. It seemed to Telly that the Tree opened before her once more, its well-remembered arms enclosing everything. But someone stood in her way. Gary Lightfoot smiled. He held up a big silver fish. The big fish gasped and struggled. Telly opened her eyes.

"What's the matter?" asked Helen.

"I can't breathe. I think I'm going to be sick."

"Come on," said Helen, "quick."

Helen Fishbone steered Telly forcefully along the corridor. Telly noted every whorl in the nasty-textured carpet as she went. Crazily angled walls made her head spin. They negotiated a doorway. Someone else's bathroom opened coldly in front of her. A horrible, alien bathroom. Everything bright and hard and shiny jumped out at her. Hard, shiny tiles. Horrible shiny faucets. An unfriendly basin and toilet. Someone else's toilet. *Home,* thought

Telly. *I want to go home. Mum. I want you. Mum.* Saliva flooded her mouth. She was drowning in Helen Fishbone's bathroom. The toilet rug was unbearably pink. If only it hadn't been that particular pink, she might—just might—have managed. For a moment, Telly held on. Then she let everything go.

It felt like someone else. Someone else being thoroughly and disgustingly sick at a friend's house. Helen hovered helplessly. Then she flushed the toilet. Telly sat back against the bathroom wall. Her feet seemed small and distant, the way they did when she came out of the cinema with her head in the clouds. Footsteps approached on the stairs. "Telly?"

"Is Telly there?" Mrs. Fishbone burst in. She took in the scene with dismay. "You poor thing. There's someone here for you, dear."

Telly watched as several things happened at once. She felt as if none of it concerned her. She'd never seen the tall man before in her life. He filled the doorway completely. Assessing the situation at a glance, he scooped her up like a doll. Race bobbed at his heels like a terrier, jumping up to babble in her face:

"I *knew* he was coming, an' he did—an' his hat blew off when we got in the car, an' guess what, Dewie was only up Home Field all the time, an' what happened was . . ."

Telly tasted sick. She licked her lips. The tall man's face looked down. His arms enclosed her kindly.

"We were chasing his hat an' we saw Dewie under the shed an' we poked him out with sticks an' he's in the back of the car. An' his hat's a bushwhacker's hat you get in a shop where you get all hunting stuff if you want—an' when we got in the car the wind almost blew the doors off an' everything, an' I said we better not go—but he said, roll over jumbo an' pass me the keys, he never came all the way from Brisbane to see us an' let an elephant's fart of a storm stop him now." Race paused for breath, bumping down the stairs. He opened the Fishbones' front door. Dad's car waited outside.

"If you're sure—" said Mrs. Fishbone. "Will she be all right?"

"No worries," quacked the tall man, in his oddly brassy voice. "No place like home if you're crook."

"Home's the best place," agreed Mrs. Fishbone, holding the door. She looked out apprehensively. "Wouldn't like to be out in a boat on a night like this, would you? Talk about those in peril on the sea. Plenty in peril tonight."

"I reckon," agreed the tall man, shouldering Telly out.

"Nice to meet you at last," called Mrs. Fishbone. "Maggie'll be thrilled."

Telly looked up in the tall man's face as he stowed her safely in the car. The tall man winked. Telly smiled. Then she closed her eyes. She'd been going around with the weight of the world on her shoulders. She hadn't slept for three days. She hadn't realized how tired she was until now. Her drowsy hand found Dewie in the footwell. She stroked him very gently back and forth. How very, very hundred-year-old tired she was . . .

The wind battered the car all the way home, but it didn't matter now. There was nothing she could do. Something had happened. Something terrible, something wonderful. There was nothing anyone could do. Not now. For those in peril, she thought, as she slipped away to sleep. For those in peril. On the sea.

8

A SHRIMP SHORT OF A BARBIE

 As soon as Telly woke up, she knew some things were changed forever. "Lightfoot," she whispered, "you there?"

Of course he was. She hadn't dreamed it. From this moment on, she had a helper. Lightfoot would direct her in everything. She felt better this morning. So much better, she couldn't help wondering what yesterday had been all about. The coming of Lightfoot, she supposed. Things as big as *that* weren't about to be easy. She washed and dressed and ran lightly downstairs through the kitchen. Once out the back door, Telly tasted the air. Rounding the corner on the battered-looking Stephenson frame, she checked the thermometers inside. About time she filed some proper reports. *Eh, Lightfoot?*

Telly marched down the slope against the wind. The blade of the damaged turbine looked sadder than ever. It had shed the rest of its cladding generously over the grass, leaving a toffee-colored polyester spine hanging in the wind like some giant dinosaur jawbone on display. The turbine would be dead until Dad fixed it. But the rest of the turbines were busy. Their giant arms tumbled around, telling the truth for once: Everything—*swish*—changes, wouldn't you—*swish*—know it?

Tricking open the fancy lock on the cubicle door of the second turbine she came to, Telly let herself in. She looked up. The great dark throat of the tower above her bonged and boomed in the wind. The ladder running up inside it dwindled away in the darkness, the cables opposite buzzed with six hundred and ninety volts. The steel walls hummed with energy, taut as a clipper under sail. Quickly paging a graph on the twin computers, Telly noted wind speeds. Not quite as strong as yesterday. But plenty strong enough.

The strangest thing, on the way back up to the house. *Hey, Lightfoot. See those parrots? There, on the phone wires. Two of them, see?* Telly ran, catching a glimpse as they winged it, one after the other, to the stunted little copse behind the house. The copse looked funny this morning. Some of the trees had got drunk in the night and needed to lean on their neighbors. Others had shown themselves up completely and fallen over. Telly watched the parrots until she couldn't see them any more, wondering where they'd escaped from. Tropical green and red, they made a brilliant flag against the pines. *The animals came in two by two,* thought Telly. It was a strange, upside-down kind of morning, like everything had gotten jumbled up in a hat in the night and drawn out willy-nilly. *Trees? Stick 'em here. Whoops. Wrong way up. Parrots? Why not?* Telly grinned. Good thing she had Lightfoot to help her. She felt pretty upside down herself. Maybe that was what happened at the end of the world. *What next?* she wondered. *Dragons?*

What was next was Greville Jackett. Clumping up the path with his nose in his coat, Mr. Jackett, thought Telly, looked more than a little dejected. A mere shadow of Super Paperboy. For some reason, he didn't have his canvas sling of papers.

Telly waited in the shelter of the porch. "What, no papers?"

Bleary and wind-blasted, Greville looked up. Telly stared. The wind had been full in his face. That's why his eyes were watering.

"No news today?"

Grev shook his head. "Printers is out. I'm goin' around tellin' it anyway."

"Telling what?"

Greville Jackett shifted his weight from one foot to the other. He dragged the back of his hand across his eyes. "I got to be careful how I tell it. Somethin' happened. Some people know 'im, some people don't."

"Is it Gary Lightfoot?"

Grev boggled. "How did you know?"

Telly hesitated. "Heard it on the radio."

"You can't have, they never gave a name. They jus' said a boy of fourteen swept to his death off the Guggles last night. They only identified his— "

Telly waited.

"Identified his body at six o'clock. I didn't know you knew Gary Lightfoot."

"Didn't know you did," said Telly.

"I won't know 'im no more," said Grev, tragically.

"Fishing, was he?"

Grev shrugged. He couldn't speak. Why do these things happen? The turbines wheeled behind them, round and round and round, no matter what else stopped. Everything—*swish*—goes on, everything—*swish*—goes on. They stood a moment in silence, sharing Gary Lightfoot.

Telly cleared her throat. "Want to come in for a drink or something?"

"No, thanks," said Grev. "I got to get on."

"I just saw parrots in the trees."

Grev nodded. "They're all over, them parrots. Cages up Amazon Park got smashed. Tree blew down on the Bird House."

The Bird House at Amazon Park. Telly remembered her one and only visit. Exotic Birds. Picnic Tables. Nature Trail. A Fun Day Out for All the Family. She pictured the scrupulously clean but sad-looking aviaries. Then she pictured the glorious

flight of the parrots, the cockatiels, lovebirds, bud-
gies, macaws, finches, and mynahs, extending their
hothouse wings, streaming away from Amazon Park
to freedom on the wind. Somehow she couldn't feel
sorry.

"Good," she said, "I hope they all escape. How
d'you know about it, anyway?"

"Giles's Newsagent. Not much Giles don't know.
It's hell up in town. There's, like, *cars* blown over.
Anyway. I better go."

Telly nodded. "Thanks for coming to tell me.
About Gary."

"How *did* you know?"

"Just a guess. I know he goes out fishing."

"I guess old Gary wished he never went out last
night."

"Don't be too sad," said Telly. Then she said:
"There's nothing to be afraid of."

Grev stared. "That's what Si said."

"Simon Elliot?"

"I was up Simon Elliot's seven o'clock last night
doin' that Weather Eye thing? With the tree? I
thought it'd be stupid, but it wasn't. An' Si goes,
'there's nothing to be afraid of,' weird kind of voice,
right after we done the tree."

Telly nodded slowly. "Coming to the meeting up
the Lookout, Friday?"

"I reckon. Someone got to stand in for 'im."

"Gary?"

"He'd've been there, wouldn't he?"

"I reckon," said Telly, softly. *Light of foot. Lightfoot. Well named, strangely changed. Be there anyway, won't you?*

Greville Jackett turned to resume his round. A paperboy without papers, he brightened a little as he went, throwing Telly a wave as he picked up his bike by the wall. Telly watched him push it. He'd jump on when he reached the village road, where the hedges would lend him protection.

Back in the kitchen, Telly helped herself to breakfast. Enormously hungry, she tanked down two bowls of cereal. Then she spread a Weetabix with peanut butter and ate it thoughtfully at the kitchen table. Something banged on the floor upstairs. Telly looked up. Only Race jumping out of bed. She put her bowl in the empty sink. No bowl from Dad's breakfast, she noticed. Usually he ate before anyone else and went on out to the turbines. Dad must still be in bed. Telly wondered hazily what time he'd gotten back last night. Everything last night was a little hazy. For some reason.

Taking a handful of Sugar Puffs, Telly wandered into the living room. Whipping open the curtains, she considered the windows behind. Funny. Someone had plastered masking tape all around the edges, and they hadn't been too fussy how they did it. It looked like a chimpanzee's idea of a proper job. It could only be Race in Draft-proofing mode.

Grinning, Telly turned. The grin died slowly. Someone was asleep on the settee. Someone whose legs stuck well out over the end of it. Someone tall. Telly swallowed her Sugar Puffs. She couldn't remember anything from the time she'd fallen asleep in the car. Now the way she'd got there began to filter back. This was her rescuer. The tall man who'd scooped her up, when she'd felt so ill she could die. For some reason, she'd forgotten the tall man entirely.

Telly walked all around him one way, then all around him the other. The tall man was real enough. She picked up his hat. WINDY'S BUSH SUPPLIES, BRENDON ST., BRISBANE, said the label inside. Australian enough, as well.

"Hey, Lightfoot, see this?" whispered Telly, turning the hat in her hand. "Windy's Bush Supplies. Wonder what it's like? Probably a big, long, dusty shop with bare floorboards and big hooks and barrels of beans and pots and pans and billy cans and boxes of nails and . . ."

The tall man opened one eye.

Still holding his hat, Telly closed hers. ". . . fishing-rods and bait and khaki trousers and canteens and hip flasks. And dusty passages full of boots and hats and traps, and—Lightfoot? Yes. I know. You like him. So do I."

Telly opened her eyes. The tall man closed one eye quickly.

"Crinkly lines around his eyes, see?" whispered Telly. "Shows he smiles a lot. I'm really glad he brought me home, you know? I don't know what I'd've done if he hadn't—"

Telly looked up. Frowzy and sleep-rumpled, Race stood listening at the door.

"What's with you?" he asked dimly.

Telly straightened. She put down the hat. "Who is he?"

Race rubbed his eyes. "I tol' you last night. He brought you home, remember?"

"Is it—"

"Uncle Race Peters, who d'you think? Only don't call him that, he likes Ray."

"Ray," said Telly, "why?"

"Ray says it's not worth havin' a handle you have to fight about. Plenty of other things to fight about. You can't have a funny name in Queensland, see? Everyone winds you up."

"Bet Windy has a hard time," grinned Telly.

"Who's Windy?"

"Windy's Bush Supplies. Where he got the hat."

The phone in the hall rang suddenly. Telly jumped. "I'll get it. They must've fixed the line."

Telly snatched the receiver. "Pell Mell 839."

"Is that Telly?"

Terrible line. It sounded like Dad, but it couldn't be. Telly raised her voice. "Who's calling, please?"

"It's Dad. Thank God, I've been trying to—"

"I'm sorry," said Telly firmly. "My father's asleep upstairs."

"Don't play games with me, Telly, I've been trying to get through all night. Is everything all right at your end?"

Dad. There was no mistaking the anxious edge to his voice. "I thought you were still in bed," said Telly. "I thought you got back last night."

"I got as far as Tarmouth. Got turned back on the bypass. Big truck blew over, apparently. Chemicals across four lanes. And flooding—all major roads closed. It's chaos. I went back and spent the night with Sven. I knew you'd be all right with Mrs. Ruddock."

"Sven?"

"Sven Hansen. At Heyderstrom Technics. Any turbine damage?"

"Don't think so," said Telly. "Mrs. Ruddock went home. You'll never guess who's here."

"No," said Dad, "I won't. I've only got thirty seconds left."

"Uncle Race!"

"Race Peters?"

"He turned up last night in the storm."

Dad took it in. "Blow me down. Race Peters. Let me speak to him, will you?"

"He's asleep on the settee."

"Never mind, I'm running out of time. Listen. If Uncle Race is there to keep an eye on things,

I may hang on here for a bit. Sven's got a new blade in stock. There might be a chance to bring it in if they open the roads later on, it'll save a lot of —"

"What about Mum?" asked Telly urgently. "I wonder if Mum's all right."

"Mum's fine. She tried to ring you last night. She's coming home just as soon as —"

Dit—dit—dit. "Say hello to Uncle Race for me, won't—" *Dit—dit.* Cut out.

Telly put the phone down thoughtfully. So far from being upstairs asleep in bed, Dad was seventy-odd miles away, the wrong side of motorway madness. She'd thought she knew where he was. Turns out she didn't know anything. Upside-down morning, or what? *You knew, didn't you, Lightfoot? Might have said. Holding out on me, huh?*

The hall thrummed as the wind changed its tone. The hall mat lifted expressively. Someone had stuffed the letterbox up with the bath sponge to keep it from rattling. They'd jammed up the gaps around the front door with towels, as well—but still the draft whistled through over the voices from the living room. Telly listened. Race and Uncle Peters— Ray—were talking:

"—and she parked it up in Home Field, where I showed you—and Dad doesn't know *anything about it,*" finished Race triumphantly.

Telly crept to the door.

"How's that?" asked Ray. "Why wouldn't you let on?"

"Tell Dad Telly took the car? He'll go mad when he finds out."

"Your Dad always was a bit of a stuffed shirt," said Ray. "I remember the day he met your mother. Mags, I said, you're looking at slow death in pants. You don't want an engineer."

"Did, though, didn't she?" Race had a grin in his voice. "'Cos then they got married."

"I'll teach you to drive," said Ray. "I drove the pickup like a pro when I was your age."

"Will you teach me? Really?"

"Go for your life. Soon as this weather calms down. Know what a bush promise is?"

Telly watched through the crack in the door. She saw Ray spit in his palm. Race did the same. Then they shook hands. The promise—the kind of promise Telly felt sure Dad would take a dim view of—was signed and sealed in a moment.

"So what's the old man driving?" asked Ray.

"He borrowed Mr. Fishbone's car. Dad thinks our car's stolen."

Ray doubled up over his sleeping bag. Strange bursting noises escaped him. When he looked up his face was red. He had Telly worried for a moment. Then she relaxed. He was laughing.

"Best crack I've heard in years. Worth coming twelve thousand miles for. Thinks it's stolen. Man's a drop-kick, can't see through his own kids—"

"My Dad's not a drop-kick. Telly tells lies and she shouldn't."

"Hey. Only pullin' your leg."

Telly knotted her fists by the crack in the door. She didn't tell lies. They might've been half-truths or silences. But she'd never actually lied. Right now though, she wouldn't mind lying. She wouldn't mind digging her fingernails into the softer parts of Race's legs and lying through her teeth about it afterward. The way she felt at the moment.

"Strange kid, your sister," said Ray. "One shrimp short of a barbie, if you ask me. What's all this light-foot guff?"

"When she was talking to herself jus' now? Dunno," said Race. "She's been funny ever since the accident."

"What accident would that be?"

"The accident with the stuff off the turbine. This, like, long strip of stuff—"

"What stuff?"

"The stuff off the turbine," explained Race patiently. "There was this big storm an' this stuff blew off on Telly an' she almost got killed. We went to the hospital an' looked at skull pictures an' the doctor goes, 'Lucky girl no fractures.' That's when she took the car."

"And parked it up in the field?"

Race nodded. "She's been, like, different ever

since. I wish she was back how she was. She won't let me join her club. She goes out places in the night—"

Enough already. Telly walked crisply in. Race was spilling enough beans to fill a bathtub.

"Who wants tea?" she asked brightly, as though she'd been bustling in the kitchen. "That was Dad on the phone. He's staying to sort out a blade for the turbine now Uncle Race—now Ray's here. He says to say hello. He couldn't get back last night because all the roads were flooded." Telly turned to Ray. "How come you managed to get here?"

"Two-forty train from Paddington. Storm hit us like a 'dozer halfway down." Ray unzipped his sleeping bag and stuck out a long, hairy leg. "Hitched a ride from the station. Never thought we'd make it up the road."

"You came out in the car and got me all the same." Telly smiled uncertainly. "You rescued me from the Fishbones."

"An' he rescued Dewie," chipped in Race. "Bet you're always rescuin' people in the outback. Bet you go days without water, huntin' and trackin' an'—"

"Hold it down," said Ray. "Don't get the wrong idea. I'm not Crocodile Dundee."

"What do you do?" asked Telly.

"Accountant. I'm what you might call a weekend bushwhacker."

"An accountant?" Telly frowned. It wasn't very glamorous.

"Hey," said Ray, "don't knock it. Number-crunching bought me a ticket to fly twelve thousand miles to see you, didn't it?"

"I guess," said Telly, smiling.

"You're bright-eyed and bushy-tailed this morning. You looked pretty green last night."

Telly shrugged. "I'm fine."

Ray poked Race. "How about some clothes, chief?"

"What?"

"How about getting dressed?"

"Oh. Okay." Race jumped up and ran out.

Ray watched him go. Then he sat up. "Your brother's a shrimp short of a barbie, isn't he? What's all this drafts guff?"

"What did he say?" asked Telly.

"I come in the door last night, he says to me, 'Uncle Race!' An' we shake on it, sweet as a nut. Then he says, 'I thought you were coming to get me. I thought you were King of the Drafts.'"

"Oh." Telly grinned. "He's always been frightened of drafts."

"Why wouldn't he be?" Ray rolled his eyes.

"Does Mum know you're here?"

Ray shook his head. "Surprise. How's she goin', anyway?"

"Mum? She's good. She's away negotiating a contract."

"That right?"

Telly nodded. "She's doing a presentation about the windfarm for Wessex Power. Then she's going to Welsh Energy and doing the same. If one of 'em likes it, they'll buy our electricity. Mum wants a twelve-month contract. I hope it's going okay. It's really important we get it. Our contract's almost up with Electric Southwest."

"No worries." Ray shrugged a pullover on. "Mags'd talk a mule clean out of his hide."

Telly passed his trousers. Thunder on the stairs. Race reappeared in jeans and a sweater. Things were coming together.

"What's the weather been like in Australia lately?" asked Telly, really wanting to know.

Ray jumped up. "Don't you kids do nothin' but talk? Let's rustle up some tucker. We got us a windfarm to run."

9

S L A U G H T E R   M I L L

For two long days the wind blew. No one went out. No one came in. Mum rang. Dad rang. Nothing changed. It was disappointing, thought Telly. She couldn't tell Mum about Ray. They'd agreed to keep the surprise. She couldn't even log into the network. The power cut meant an end to any messages; the end of any link to global Weather Eye, for the while. The house stayed stubbornly dark. So did the TV. Gloom clotted in corners as thundering night followed thundering day. Race grew steadily jumpier. So did Ray, after Telly flushed his cigarettes down the toilet. She spared him the details. And the health-care lecture. He'd come all the way from Down Under. He would need a day or two to settle in.

Ray settled in over Clue. Sucking a matchstick, he played his cards close to his chest. Too close. Telly consulted the rules. You couldn't sit on suspects, she insisted, crossly. If you had Professor Plum when someone asked, you had to show you had him.

"Take the old bludger then," Ray said. "I'll trade him for half a ciggie."

"That's not the way you play it."

"Way I play it," said Ray.

Race grinned. Ray was outrageous. He made up his own rules for everything. He showed them Squeeze the Monkey. Squeeze the Monkey was a card game that involved Telly and Race betting a stack of chocolate biscuits Ray wouldn't win. But Ray always won. Pretty soon he'd squeezed the monkey dry. Telly made a shopping list. They were running low on biscuits. And just about everything else.

For two long days the living room boomed like a kettledrum. Mrs. Ruddock popped in for company. She chattered nervously a long while, throwing glances at Ray. This wind. Made you think you were going mad. Doctor said her nerves were on a knife-edge. She didn't know how she could have done it, she'd been sewing thirty-five years. She'd taken two of her nerve pills directly when she got in. What must Mr. Peters think? A hole in her frock like that. Mrs. Ruddock brought out a shopping list and hid herself behind it. Would they mind picking up a few groceries? Whenever they were going down the village? She could do with a few cans of cat food. Toby was living off corned beef. She wouldn't ask, only she couldn't get out in this wind.

Ray took her list and teased her a little. One tub, slimline marg. How about two tubs, slimline marg—make her twice as slim? He couldn't believe Mrs. Ruddock needed six individual apple pies. Or A1 sauce. Saucy enough, already. Mrs. Ruddock flushed. Mr. Peters was wicked—wasn't he? She went home somewhat cheered.

Both mornings Telly and Ray fought their way out to the turbines. On instructions from Dad, Ray climbed up to each cabin and checked out the braking system. Without it the blades would turn faster and faster until they thrashed themselves to pieces. Telly watched anxiously until she saw his legs emerging from the darkness at the top of the ladder. The hydraulic brakes would be taking quite a hammering. She checked the wind-speed monitors. They recorded a cutout both nights when the wind had topped force ten.

Both afternoons Telly and Race watched Ray tinkering with the evil old generator in the shed. A standby from the dim and distant days before electricity had reached South Hill—when the windfarm had been little more than a twinkle in Dad's eye—it resisted every effort to bring it to life. Ray's language grew colorful. He had, thought Telly, a pretty sweeping turn of phrase—embracing not only the generator on the bench and every other generator that had ever been manufactured, but the whole idea of generators in general and the parentage of the original inventor. Race rehearsed every phrase under his breath for future reference. The generator sat mutely in the shed. It looked as though Ray would generate electricity before it did.

"Crazy pom setup," grumbled Ray. "Turbines cranking out juice like an express train outside, not enough power in the house to warm a mozzie's backside. Makes about as much sense as anything else around here."

"We never had a power cut like *this* before," Telly said defensively.

"That'd be right."

"Anyway. All our electricity goes to the substation. The substation sends it out."

"Not here, it doesn't."

"No," said Telly. "Too many power lines down."

"Why couldn't we, like, get wires from the turbines an' get wires from the house," Race knotted his fingers expressively, "an', like, join 'em together an' make the kettle boil?"

Telly looked at Race witheringly. "Because we'd burn the house down. High voltage, dummyhead."

When they weren't watching Ray bloody his knuckles on the old generator, they rattled around in the cold, dark house together—like peas in a drum, Ray said. Ray said he might as well sleep on the pullout in the old back bedroom. Race explained earnestly and at length how the Drafts would get him while he was asleep if he did. The window in the old back bedroom didn't close properly, they'd get in for sure. They'd gotten in once before. Ray listened carefully. Then he went up to the back bedroom and made up the pullout.

Both evenings at seven o'clock precisely, alone in her booming bedroom, Telly did the Tree. Each time it came a little easier. Lightfoot showed her the way. Each time she found the Tree in the Meadow, she touched an immeasurable calm. It seemed to Telly that the hour had a special note. The stillness at seven o'clock was of a kind found only in big, solemn places where very many people had bent their minds together. It was better than any network. Many people—very many people—were Calming all over the world. Everyone was helping. She could feel it.

Friday afternoon the wind dropped a little. Telly stood at the living room window watching Ray back up the car to the door. Getting the car for the meeting that night at the Lookout wasn't going to be the easiest trick in the world. Ray was pretty loose, but she guessed he'd have something to say about her driving off at midnight. Telly's anxiety rose. She'd wanted to network a message. The mood would be down after Gary's death. Would anyone show up at Bready Lookout? It was important they did. Something had happened. Lightfoot would help her explain. She listened a moment. *Nice one,*

Lightfoot. Good idea. One way to make sure they come.

"Grocery run! Now!" Ray hollered in through the door.

Telly climbed thoughtfully into the car beside Ray. Race bombed in last of all. Then he got out again and closed the front door of the house.

"Hear you drive pretty good," Ray said conversationally. "Like to swap places and take her down the lane?"

"Not much," said Telly coldly.

Plenty of time—eh, Lightfoot? Plenty of time for driving. Tonight. When the wind is up.

Pink and white squashy Dog Bones (suck 'em up with straws), Gummy Spiders (purple-red and green), mallow Dinosaurs, Fizbombs (really strong), Fried Eggs, Traffic Lights (red, yellow, green), Red Bootlaces—about a million for a penny. Flumps, Frogslegs, Cola Bottles, Midget Gems, Circus Peanuts, Nibbles, Dorks, Pop Ups, Dummies, Double Ducks, Gummy Motorbikes, white and brown chocolate eggs, and Kola Krackles.

Race licked his lips. Giles's Newsagent and Stores had the best selection of penny sweets this side of paradise. Hovering over the plastic trays and sugar-dusted screw-top bottles, his paper bag carefully widened with his fist, Race popped in twelve circus peanuts. Then he changed his mind. Glancing at Mrs. Giles serving Ray at the counter, he took six of them out again and popped in six Fried Eggs. Twelve pence so far. What else? Six more Fried Eggs, for a start. You couldn't get Fried Eggs everywhere. Then, probably, six Dinosaurs, coupla Fizbombs, two Traffic Lights, one or two Pop Ups, a dozen Frogslegs and Dog Bones, mixed. Plus a few Flumps and a Double Duck. He had sixty-eight pence. He could use up the rest on Bootlaces. Except he needed twelve pence for Kola Krackles. Race sighed. Deciding was the difficult bit. You could go mad in Giles's with sixty-eight pence. You could pig out until you were sick and still have enough left over for a whole mess of red licorice Bootlaces. Why shop anywhere else? Anyone, thought Race, could eat like a king in Giles's.

Telly packed groceries into three big carrier bags at the counter. They'd bought some funny things, she noticed. Canned shrimp and frozen steak. Yuk. A packet of iced ginger slices. They never bought iced ginger slices. Two six-packs of Gold Seal Extra Strong Lager. Two packs of Benson & Hedges. Telly left the cigarettes until last. She looked at Ray. Ray was blithely ordering Mrs. Ruddock's list, further up near the register. Telly flicked the packets of cigarettes neatly off the other side of the counter. What Ray hadn't got, he would have to do without. *Good thing too,* thought Telly crossly. Iced Ginger Slices. No one even *liked* ginger except him. At least they had bread, milk, tea, cheese, and eggs. And orange juice and toilet paper. She supposed it could've been worse.

Hefting the bags across the shop, Telly propped them against the sandbags by the door and waited for Ray to finish. The village street outside was still under an inch or two of water. Judging by the tide-mark under the pub windows opposite, it had been under a good six inches or more, not so very long ago either. Piles of filthy debris in the gutters. Sand-bags at every door. DAY SIX OF HURRICANE HELL shouted the headlines from leader boards on the pavement. WEST FACES BLACKOUT AS POWER CRISIS LOOMS.

"Stop 'ome and sit tight," Mrs. Giles was telling Ray. "That's what they're giving out on the radio. I said to Jack, that's a joke. You can't do nothin' else."

"No newspapers?" Ray asked.

Mrs. Giles shook her head. "Still waiting." She pointed to a handwritten announcement at the till:

> CORNISH PRESS FEDERATION REGRETS
> NO LOCAL PAPERS DUE TO STORM
> DAMAGE TO PRINT WORKS. NORMAL
> SERVICE WILL BE RESUMED ASAP.

"I got a local newsletter," offered Mrs. Giles. "Here. 'Porth Madder boy drowned in night of terror.' Terrible business, isn't it? Just about broke my heart."

"I wouldn't know," Ray said. "I only just arrived."

"Ah, then you wouldn't. Lovely lad he was, too."

Telly swallowed. Everywhere in people's minds, nowhere in their sights. *Except mine. Filmy, quicksilver Lightfoot. If only they knew how you'd changed.*

Ray finished up. They splashed across the street and swung the groceries into the car. Ray went back for more. At last all the bags were in the trunk. The wind smelled sick outside. Like school toilets. Or sewage. The flood must have flushed out the drains.

"Got the batteries for the radio?" Telly asked.

Ray nodded. "Where's the candy king? Still inside?"

They watched the newsagent's door. Presently, Race wandered out, absorbed in his penny selection. Fresh from Planet Gross Out, he looked around, remembering where he was.

"Take your time," called Telly, cuttingly.

Race bobbed smoothly into the car. It was impossible to rile him after the Giles's Selection Counter Experience. Ray jumped in behind the wheel. He revved up and waited for Telly.

Telly leaned in at the window. "I think I'll stay in the village a bit. There's someone I want to see."

"Go for your life. Who is it?"

"Someone. I'll get a lift back. Won't be long."

"Look. I have to know where you are. Don't I?"

Telly hesitated. "It's Crippen's place. Slaughter

Mill. Just down the lane by the Primary School."

Race looked up. Telly. Visiting Crips. He could hardly believe his ears.

"Jump in, I'll drop you off," offered Ray.

Race cleared his throat. "Telly loves Crips—"

"No thanks, I'd rather walk."

"Crips loves Telly—"

"Shut it," glared Telly.

"Or you'll kiss me to death?" Race made out with his arm. "Oh, kiss me, Crips, I love you. Oh, darlin' Crips, I—"

"Can we leave his body to science after we kill him?" Telly asked Ray.

Ray looked doubtful. "Wouldn't want it, would they? Too many chemical additives."

Once past Pell Mell Primary, Telly quickened her step. Walking in wellies was a drag. Must be half a mile to Slaughter Mill. Half a mile of mud puddles. Slaughter Mill was called Slaughter Mill because of some obscure Celtic scuffle, back when mills had mattered. Some party had ambushed some other party and outnumbered them three to one. The mill-stream had run red, supposedly.

"Even today, a strange atmosphere pervades the killing floor at Slaughter Mill," said the standard guide to the parish every local child had studied at length in school. "The visitor will be well advised to pause a while and reflect on our turbulent heritage."

Slaughter Mill was the kind of place you'd expect Terry Crippen to live.

Pity the primary school was out of action, thought Telly, nearing the neatly restored mill house at last. The damage to the school had looked pretty extensive. Race would be home forever. Bet *she* wouldn't. Bet Mrs. Yardley would open Roadford Community High School just as soon as they fixed up the power lines. Mrs. Yardley was like that. Telly could see Mrs. Yardley's favorite pupil out on the drive ahead. Crips looked up. Then he looked down again. He wasn't about to acknowledge Telly's approach.

Telly crunched in on the drive. Then she stopped. "What's that?"

"Mountain bike, what's it look like?"

"I mean, why's it all in pieces?"

Crips straightened, wiping his hands on his jeans. One wheel on, one wheel off, the mountain bike looked sad. Its pedals, chain, and brake cables had been neatly arranged on the grooved granite mill-stone that made a centerpiece for the drive.

"I'm strippin' it down for a paint job. Probably spray it black."

Telly nodded. "Classy."

Taking the saddle in both hands, Crips wrenched it from side to side. Telly watched, glad it wasn't her bike Crips was cannibalizing. Whose was it, anyway?

It wasn't his. Crips had a Green Flash All Terrain Roughrider, and he never let anyone forget it. Who'd be stupid enough to let Crips get his hands on their bike?

"Here." Telly peered under the saddle. "You want to undo this nut."

"I knew that." Crips flushed. "I'm only loosenin' it up." Turning away he fiddled out a wrench from a wallet on the millstone. He checked the size and swapped it coolly for another.

Telly held the saddle as Crips worked the nut. "You know the meeting tonight—"

"I got to hand it to you." Crips met her eyes over the bike frame. His own eyes were curious blue. "You said something was goin' to happen. Somethin' happened all right."

"Yeh?" Telly waited. *Lightfoot, you snake. Been visiting Crips, have you, too?*

"You won't say nothin', will you? Dad says don't spread it. Put people off buyin' the house."

"What will?"

Crips lowered his voice conspiratorially. "Get this. You know the other night we lost the roof off our extension? Well, anyway—same night, the mill-stream comes up in the kitchen, water everywhere, an' get this: bones. Like, old bones from when they done the slaughter? Must've been under the floor like in *Tomb of the Evil Dead*. Real horror-show job, Mum does her head in."

"Sick." Telly listened. It was no surprise. Whichever way she turned lately there was the Grim Reaper, singing the same old song. He was pretty much a one-note wonder.

"Gran goes, What did I tell you? Judgement day, the dead's comin' out of their graves. Dad goes, Get back in bed, you daft old kettle. Next night, top of the old chimney stack falls down the chimney in the fireplace. Gran goes, It's a sign. Dad goes, Sign you shut up." Crips paused. "Mill wheel's jus' about blown off the side of the house. Could go anytime. It's unreal. How'd you know it was coming?"

"This weather?" Telly shrugged. "Forecast gave it out."

"Not like this, they never. Old Cummins—know Cumminses?—Cummins's horse-box blew over Wednesday night and done in his new Volvo." Crips shook his head. "It's helluva lot worse than they said."

"About the meeting—"

"An' that tree thing on the computer. You send it out?"

"Did you do it? But you're not on the Weather Eye network."

"I am now. Simon Elliot sends me this access code, so I get the message, right? Old Si says give it a go, me an' Grev done it, it's smart. So I sit down seven o'clock the other night, right? An' I'm thinkin' about the match next Saturday when I get this tree in my head and I'm feelin' all—" Crips looked sheepish "—peaceful an' everything. Next thing, I'm looking at the clock an' it's half past seven! Like, half an hour—an' it feels like I jus' sat down. Good buzz," he added thoughtfully.

Even Crips, thought Telly. The wonderful tree had a long and surprising reach.

"Think anyone'll turn up tonight?"

"Up Bready Lookout? Me, for one." Crips finished unscrewing the nut under the saddle with his fingers.

"I'm worried no one'll come. 'Specially after Gary."

"It sucks, what happened to Gary." Crips jerked the saddle off and set it down on the millstone. He wiped his face with his sleeve. "This is Gary's bike."

Telly stared. "How come?"

"David Henry gave it to me."

"David Henry? Why?"

"Reminded him too much of Gary."

"How did David Henry get Gary Lightfoot's bike?" asked Telly patiently.

"Gary's dad gave it him. Gary's dad said he didn't care what he did with it, jus' take it away, he never wanted to see it again in his life. Old Gary went out on it the night he drowned."

Lightfoot, thought Telly, *you listening? The things people do. The silly, sad things people do. Especially the people who love you.*

"Then what?" she asked.

"Then David Henry keeps it. Then he gets spooked. He gets so he doesn't want to use it. After a day or two he cycles over here an' asks me if I want it. Like, what am I goin' to say?" Crips spread his arms expressively. "No? To a free bike?"

"Free?"

Crips nodded. "'Sell it,' he goes. 'Or keep it. I don't want to see it no more. It's like Gary's hangin' around me every time I ride it.' So first I thought I'd keep it. Then last night I start thinkin' about old Gary. About how he rides off that night and never comes back. How this bike's prob'ly the last thing he touches on dry land. Then I start thinkin' about drownin'. About what drownin's like." Crips swallowed. "So now I think I'll do it up an' sell it."

Telly nodded slowly. "Think Gary's brother'll come tonight?"

"Sam Lightfoot?" Crips shrugged. "Dunno."

"What about David Henry? It's really important. They've all got to come. I want you to go around and tell them."

"Me? Why?"

"They'll listen to you. Followed you up the Edge, didn't they? Get Hughie Pridham as well. Get everyone. Say it's for Gary. Please."

Crips looked doubtful. "I dunno. I s'pose I could round 'em up. Dunno if they'll come."

Telly looked Crips in the eye. "Make them come," she told him.

10

B U S H   C A M P   I N

T H E   B A C K   B E D R O O M

One thing, indicated Lightfoot. If anyone interrupted her, her heart would stop and she'd die. That was the only thing. Telly bounded smoothly on. No one would interrupt her.

Fast Walking was a useful way to get from A to B. She wished he'd shown her before. What you did was, you chose a word. Then you emptied your mind and let the word carry you over the fields. The three miles between Slaughter Mill and South Hill disappeared easily under Telly's bounding feet.

It was teatime when she got in. The house was dead as a church. Telly sat down at the kitchen table and let go of the word repeating itself like a tape loop inside her. Her mind filled slowly with everyday things. The lighted candles by the cooker. The shopping. The teapot. Two cups of half-drunk tea. A packet of iced ginger slices. Telly breathed deeply, letting the world flood back. She gave herself plenty of time. Fast Walking wasn't something you took lightly.

Shouts of laughter filtered down from the landing. Telly made herself a cup of tea. Then she took it upstairs. The candle on the landing windowsill cast freak-show shadows on the walls. Telly felt tired of darkness. Would anything ever be clear? She cocked her head and listened. Thumping in the old back bedroom. Sounded like a riot.

Telly pushed the door. "Race? Race, you there?"

Mid-bounce under a sheet in the center of his bed, Race changed direction and plumped onto the floor. He slid out. Mildly purple around the edges, he looked at Telly.

Telly stared. "Why's your bed in here? What on earth are you doing?"

"I drove the car all the way down the lane on the way home, I did," Race announced irrelevantly. "*An'* we got an ESN."

"A what?"

"An Emergency Shutdown Notification." Ray emerged from behind the sheet he was inexplicably stringing up at the other end of the room. "Substation's blown. System's goin' crazy—too much power, no way to send it."

"How long for?"

"Engineer said all windfarms got an ESN till they re-route the power through the grid. Or fix up the power lines. Whichever."

"Better shut down, then," said Telly. "Dad won't be pleased."

"No worries, we done it. Tie up your end will ya, chief?"

Race jumped up on a chair by the wall. He looped the end of Ray's string neatly over a hook in a beam. Then he pulled. The string tautened under the ceiling, bringing two king-size bed sheets with it. The old back bedroom was strangely transformed. The sheet-tent quivered over the beds. The rest of the furniture had been carelessly shunted to the back of the room, except for a single table. With a candle. And a flash-light. And Race's Action Heroes Thermos. Between the beds stood a cooler.

"What on earth are you doing?"

Ray winked. "Camping out, aren't we, chief?"

"It's a bush camp," Race explained excitedly. He looked, thought Telly, slightly crazed. "A bush camp in the back bedroom. An' Ray says we c'n make damper in the morning. What damper is, is you get flour an' water, then you — "

"A bush camp in the back bedroom. And you're sleeping here tonight?"

Race nodded. "Then you mix it flat like pancakes, then you have this — "

"But you never sleep in the back bedroom."

"He does now," Ray said. "Any more tea in the pot?"

"You have this, like, hot griddle. An' you drop 'em on an' turn 'em."

Telly looked coldly at Race. "Jus' don't come running to me when you're scared."

"Hey," said Ray, "who's scared?"

"He is. He never even comes in here."

Ray held Telly's eyes. His own were coolly critical. "Time we hit the kitchen."

"What?"

"I'm hungry," said Ray. "Aren't you?"

After the evening meal—steak and shrimp-dressed salad—Telly read for an hour or two in the armchair. Ray asked her if she'd seen the cigarettes he'd bought. Had she packed them in the groceries or what? Telly widened her eyes. No, she hadn't. Hadn't he? Ray turned away. Let me guess. You left 'em behind on purpose. Bonzer way to drive me up the wall. Up the wall if you want them, Telly told him severely.

Ray fetched the table-tennis paddles. He and Race played a no-holds-barred candle-lit tournament over the living room table. Telly threw the ball in sourly, whenever it came her way. She wasn't exactly flavor of the month with Ray. All his jokes were for Race. Telly snapped her book and wandered on up to her room. Let them sleep in the old back bedroom. What did she care? She wouldn't even be here when the Drafts stroked Race, softly, in his sleep. When he woke in a panic and rushed in for comfort, her bed would be empty. She would be out in the wild wind, with all those wild enough to join her.

Telly felt thoroughly out of sorts and cross with herself. She'd actually read through seven o'clock Calming. How could she have forgotten? Tonight, of all nights? The notice beside her bed didn't make her feel any better. TELLY 4 CRIPS it announced, in Race's felt-tip capitals. Another notice taped to the computer said: Crips 4 Telly TRUE LOVE.

Big yuks, thought Telly. She marched smartly into Race's room and strung up Gonzo the frog with a length of red wool. She attached a distressing note: "Dear Race, Can't stand you any more. By the time you read this I'll be . . ." Gonzo's suicide note ended despairingly in a squiggle. Telly pinned his note to his green plastic chest and surveyed the effect. Childish, but satisfying. Mildly surprised, Gonzo the frog dangled from the end of Race's bookshelves. The red wool around his neck bit deeply into his fluff. Gonzo was Race's favorite. He was ready to kill if anyone stroked his nylon fur the wrong way.

Back in her room, Weather Eye lay on her bed and crossed her arms like an Egyptian mummy. The wind boomed dully outside. Whatever it said tonight escaped her. After a while she heard Race running the tap in the bathroom, cleaning his teeth with his scummy little novelty toothbrush. When would a quarter to twelve come around? Heady, breakneck, wind-in-the-teeth action was what she needed most. She'd felt strong and right and powerful ever since the Tree in the Meadow. Now she felt wrong. Even

Lightfoot had nothing to say. How could you tick a ghost off?

Ray stumped slowly up the stairs, joshing Race, throwing himself down on the pullout in the back bedroom. Race burst out on the landing and smacked her bedroom door. "Pigface cowbrain, don't you *never* touch Gonzo again."

"Wouldn't want to, he smells," Weather Eye rallied half-heartedly. Wrong and nasty, thumped her head. Might as well be wronger.

The bush camp settled feverishly. Weather Eye listened a long while in the corridor, like the outcast she was. *Like a dingo or something,* she thought. *Like a hungry yellow dingo, drinking in smells where the campfire glow meets the night.*

"Want a Fried Egg?" Race sounded flat through the sheet tent.

"Sure you can spare 'em?" Ray had a grin in his voice.

"There's Double Ducks an' Bootlaces left, as well. I ate all the Kola Krackles."

"Pass 'em over, I'll give it a go." A sweet-bag rustle. "Phew. What d'you call these?"

"Dog Bones. Me 'n' Tommy Rowe, we suck 'em up with straws. This is jus' like a real camp, isn't it? Like, a camp in the outback with billy cans an' stuff?" A pause. "What's it like in Australia?"

"Weird summer this year. Ozone's thin as a rag. Clap on your hat, slick on the sunblock, no worries. Even the sheep wear shades."

"They do? I mean—really wear sunglasses?"

"No kidding. They look pretty good in Raybans."

A long silence. Then bedsprings. Someone turning over. Someone sitting up.

"What's eating you?" Ray's voice, suddenly. "You're jumpier'n a cricket."

Vague chomping. More rustling. The darkness of the corridor folded around Telly like a helmet. The voices dimmed. She could hardly be bothered, now, to understand what they said.

"Well?"

"I'm afraid of the dark." A very small voice indeed. "Dark things in corners, waiting to jump out an' get me. Were you ever?"

"Ever what?"

"Ever afraid of things like that? When you were a kid?"

"I guess. Everyone's afraid of something."

"What are you afraid of?"

"Afraid I'll chuck if I eat any more of these Dog Bones. Sorry. Lemme see—I'm afraid of Lofty Unwin. Big lug from Hullabaloo, always had it in for me."

"And you're scared of him? I mean, really, really scared?"

"Too right. Stands about six five, muscles like a beach party in a pair of tights, touchy as a two-year-old. Scares the pants off me, but I wouldn't let him know it."

"You wouldn't?"

"Big mistake to let him know you're scared. That's what he wants, see? When I meet Lofty Unwin, I front up like he bothers me less'n a squashed fly on a tin hat. That way I don't let him get to me. See, *acting* like you're not afraid's almost the same thing as *not* being afraid. Think about it."

Race thought about it. Telly dozed in the corridor. The conversation rose and fell in her head like the burble of some party she wished she'd never gone to. Her head dropped back against the wall.

"These Drafts you're scared of." Ray again, softly. "If you act like you're not, pretty soon you won't be."

"Won't be what? Afraid?"

"Who's afraid?" Ray, quick as lightning.

"I . . . I don't know."

"I said, who's afraid?"

"Oh," said Race. "Not me."

"Bigger. *Who's afraid?*"

"Not me!"

"Go for your life!" whooped Ray.

The smile in his uncle's voice warmed Race like a big red Australian sun. It was OK to be scared of silly things. It was OK to admit it. What was he afraid of, really? Maybe Ray was right. Maybe pretending they weren't afraid was what brave people did. That was what made them brave. Race lay thinking under the sheet tent a long time after Ray's beery snores had settled into a serious rhythm. He watched the corners of the old back bedroom darken with all the horrors he thought might be in them. Then he went and stood in one. It wasn't so bad. What was he afraid of? Nothing more than the feeling. The feeling of being afraid.

Race thought a moment. Then he checked his watch. Creeping softly out he almost fell over Telly, oddly asleep in the corridor. He supposed she knew what she was doing. He poked her once and hopped the stairs. It wasn't until he opened the front door on the night-crisp, moon-flooded drive outside that Race knew what it was that he wasn't afraid to do.

The bush camp in the back bedroom had stamped out its cheery glow of small talk when Telly lifted her head. Someone poked her. Where was she? How long had she been asleep? What kind of time was it, anyway? Telly fetched her flashlight. 11:52!! Shoes! Coat! Car keys! Car keys? Telly lunged in the back bedroom and whipped Ray's jeans off the floor. Car keys, left-hand pocket. Yes! Thunderbirds are go!

Telly flung herself down the stairs and into the car. She revved up recklessly, swung around the drive, roared off in third up the lane, adjusting her lights as she went. She didn't care whether half of Pell Mell heard her coming or not. Tonight, of all nights! Late!

Don't leave me now, she thought. *Lightfoot. I know I'm wrong-headed and cross. I know I'm blowing it, somehow. If I've only got one night as Weather Eye—let it be tonight.*

11

T H E   L O O K O U T

 Helen Fishbone was waiting anxiously by the crippled old milk-churn stand at the end of Foghanger Lane.

"Where've you *been*? It's almost twelve already."

"I fell asleep. Get in."

Helen opened the passenger door. In the same moment a figure erupted out of the bushes behind her, flung itself past her and ducked into the car. Tall and dark and wholly unwelcome, it sat in the front seat and grinned.

Helen thumped it. "Denny. I hate you. Get out."

"Make me."

"You're not coming to the meeting."

"*You* say."

"Get in," said Telly impatiently. "We haven't got time for this."

"He'll ruin it. You don't know what he's like."

"Won't be anything to ruin if we don't get on."

"I hate him. Make him get out."

"What is this, playgroup or something?" Telly rounded on Denny. "Move, or we're not going anywhere."

Denny made a move to get out. "Fine," he told Helen. "I'll just tell Mum you're off now. Or did you tell her already?"

"I'm in the front with Telly." Helen knew when she was beaten. "Get out and sit in the back."

"You."

"Get in the back or we sit here all night," said Telly wearily.

Denny folded his arms. "Your uncle knows you got the car, does he? I 'spect Mum'll ring him when I tell her you drove off with Helen."

Telly engaged first gear. "Belt up," she told him shortly.

Bready Lookout loomed large on their horizon within minutes of leaving Pell Mell. An unexpected granite outcrop shaped like a volcano—which at some time it probably had been—it commanded an unbroken view between the neighboring village of Mount Oak and the sea. As the highest point for miles, it had a colorful history. In times of dire emergency it had been lighted as a beacon. It had blazed in the Civil War, when Cornwall had stood for the King. It had blazed, once, in 1943, when an enemy landing had threatened. Fire on the Lookout woke memories in those who remembered the war. Long before bombers and air raids, when a good nose for trouble meant the difference between a tidy profit from smuggling and an untidy death by the rope, Mother Bready had walked the Lookout in her crimson-lined cloak.

Whenever a French-rigged ship breached the Guggles and nosed toward Zennen Haven, Mother Bready went a-walking—or so the story went. If the day smelled clear of customs men, Mother Bready saw no reason not to take a conspicuous stroll on the Lookout in her devil black cloak. Then there would be a landing and a running of furtive men up the cliffs, and a nightcap of sea-smelling spirits for the dauntless dame herself. But if the day were chilly and thick with the whiff of preventive-men, Mother Bready would turn her crimson-lined cloak inside out for warmth, and walk the Lookout boldly in red-for-danger scarlet. Then the captain of the French-rigged ship would snap up his telescope and drown his casks on a weighted line to be grappled up sometime safer—and nose away on the tide. Many a careful captain had raised a glass to Mother Bready and her danger-red cloak in his time.

Brandy for the parson, thought Telly. *Baccy for the clerk.* The wizened old oak on the Lookout had looked down on a thing or two in its time. But not any more. The familiar shape on the skyline was missing. Some kind of monster orchid bloomed on the hill in its place. Grinding up the approach road in second gear, Telly tried to make sense of what she saw. Poor old tree was upside down. The hurricane had thrown it down like a rag, leaving its roots in the ground. The torn-off, trumpet-mouthed trunk pointed upwards at forty-five degrees like some kind of deep-throated flower. The Wizzen Tree's three hundred-odd glory days were over. Old Mother Bready was supposed to have planted it. Or had she been hung from it? One or the other. Telly could never remember.

Leaving the car on the slope above Cudlip's Quarry—where the granite had been blasted for monumental stone when monumental stone had been favored—Helen and Telly started up the path. Denny followed slowly. Telly looked up. The ageless snout of Bready Lookout nosed the moonlit sky. Lightfoot had company tonight. Pilgrims, lovers, smugglers, suicides—all had passed this way at one time or another.

"Hear that?" Helen turned. "That like, thumping noise?"

Telly listened. "Sounds like it's coming from the car."

Flooding back past Denny, they cautiously circled the car. Telly looked at Helen. "There's someone in the trunk."

The thumping inside it redoubled. Helen looked at Telly. "Open it, then," she said.

Telly threw open the trunk and jumped away like

a cat. Nothing more surprising or terrifying arose from it than Race Craven's head.

"Din' you hear me shouting?" he asked crossly. "I've jus' about shouted my *head* off."

For a moment Telly was speechless. Then she made up for it. "What are you, braindead? Don't you *know* never to shut yourself in things? How could you even think about getting in the trunk?"

"You'd never've let me come, else." Race climbed out. He rubbed his head. "Hi, Helen."

"Pretty stupid," said Helen. "What if we hadn't heard you?"

"I meant to leave it open a crack, but it never——"

"Never what?"

"Never stayed open. I never meant to shut it."

"Famous last words," said Telly. "Where d'you keep your brains these days? Under the bed with Gonzo? Have you even got any? Have you even——"

"He's okay," said Helen. "Come on."

Denny was halfway up already. Helen followed briskly. Telly swiped at Race a couple of times, but he bounced back grinning, like a ball. Irritation Factor Ten. It was nothing a really good pinch wouldn't fix. Telly's fingers itched. How did he know about the meeting?

"How did you know about the meeting?"

Race tapped his nose. "Mind your own, dog-breath." Then he ran on ahead.

"Dogbreath yourself."

The Lookout / 151

"Dogbreath back," Race called.

"Always one more dogbreath than your dog-breath," finished Telly, lapsing into playgroup mode. Annoying little swine. Probably he'd seen the message on Helen's bedroom wall. They'd probably looked in Helen's room, the night he'd come in with Ray. That was how he knew about the meeting. Telly pictured him bumping along in the trunk— shut in, alone, in the dark. She wouldn't like it herself. How had Race had the nerve? Ever since Ray came he'd been up like a spring in the mornings, insufferably cocky all day. The post-Ray Race was different altogether from the fearful little toerag scared of Drafts that Telly knew so well—different, and twice as annoying. She'd almost rather've had him how he was. At least he'd been easy to—manipulate. Telly swallowed. Not a pleasant word.

The Yellow Trail took all her concentration. Diverging wooden posts with blue and yellow arrows marked nature trails one and two. The Blue Trail wound right around the hill, biting its tail at Cudlip's Quarry, under the slope where they'd left the car. The Yellow Trail led to the summit. The rootless wreck of the Wizzen Tree ducked away behind moss-studded overhangs as Telly climbed. Halfway up she turned. Crossways Windpark stood idle and threadlike against the whistling northern horizon. Away to the southwest, the cliffs bulked dimly into the sea at the Edge.

As Telly neared the summit, the sound of David Henry holding forth about the weather fell tonelessly over the rocks.

". . . a typical mid-Atlantic depression. Then what happens is, the air over the sea gets much warmer than normal because of the jetstream blowing much farther south than it usually does, so you get this great big — "

"What's the jetstream?" Sounded like Grev.

"The jetstream's this belt of winds about twelve kilometers above sea level. So you get this huge great depression developing — "

"Why was the jetstream further south than usual?"

"Because it *was*, all right? So this depression picks up moisture from the sea as it goes along, an' no one knows it's developing, right, because there's, like, only two weather ships left in the Atlantic, an' it misses them. So anyway, the storm travels east to the Bay of Biscay. Then it takes off and heads northeast towards England—an' the computer models don't show rapid storm development because they're not getting any feedback from planes in the area, 'cos all the planes are avoiding it. So no one really rates it— an' that's how they forecast this hurricane wrong."

Telly crested the last rise separating her from the huddled group under the Wizzen Tree. Even in death, it offered some kind of protection. Handspringing on its fallen branches, the shaggy old carcass thrusted its broken root-bloom some fifteen meters in the air. They were all there, under it—all except poor Sam Lightfoot. David Henry, Crips, Si, Grev—even Hughie Pridham. With her and Helen, seven, counted Telly. With Lightfoot—in spirit—eight. Then there was Denny. And Race. They'd been busy while they waited, noted Telly. Someone had thought of a campfire. The age-dried pile of oak bark wouldn't take much lighting. Telly acknowledged Crips. "Nice one. Sorry we're late." Crips held her eyes a moment longer than he should have. He'd got them all there like she'd asked him to, hadn't he? All except grieving Sammy Lightfoot, and no one could get to *him* until after the funeral. Telly turned away. With his straw-pale hair and his all-season tan, Crips was a looker—but so was a rock python. Crips 4 Telly. Puh-lease.

Simon Elliot cleared his throat. "Calming was good tonight, wasn't it? If you're into it, I mean. I don't do it every night," he added nervously.

"I done it," said Crips. "Stone gone till seven thirty-five. When I went to get up, the room went small. Weird feeling, or what?"

"I've had that," said Grev. "Feels like you're ten feet tall."

"Had that one where you're looking down on yourself?" asked Si. "Like, when you're somewhere up near the ceiling?"

"No way." Crips stared. "Have you?"

"Nah," said Simon quickly. "It's just, I wondered

if you had." He looked away, embarrassed.

Denny scowled. "What *is* this Calming, anyway?"

"Make a circle." Telly sat down on the tail of her coat. "I want to talk about Gary."

"I still don't see it." David Henry shook his head.

Telly looked up. "See what?"

"Gary. Why would he go out on the rocks that night? Wasn't fishing weather. Way too hairy off the Guggles, anyway. He knew that. Doesn't make any sense."

"Don't think about it," said Grev. "Only makes it worse."

"The weather killed Gary," said David Henry bitterly.

"Maybe." *Why* did *he go out,* wondered Telly.

"It almost killed *you,*" said Helen Fishbone.

Something terrible, something wonderful. It wasn't going to be easy to explain. Telly waited. At last they were all sitting down. Simon avoided Denny. Denny avoided everyone else. He ended up in an awkward cusp between Race's knee and a branch. Race entered enthusiastically into the spirit of the thing. He had no difficulty with meetings under fallen trees on high and windswept spots in the night. The grassy depression he'd spotted halfway up would make, he thought, a pretty good site for a bush camp. He would have to bring Ray up to see it.

David Henry ignited the fire. The dry bark banged like crackers as the flames bit. The flames flickered, then steadied, throwing up a homely glow on the leeward side of the tree. Race drew close—too close. Appointing himself its minder, he rearranged the fire.

David Henry frowned. "Leave it alone, why don't you? You'll put it out in a minute."

Race looked at him scornfully. He added a tusk of bark to the flames. *Small bits is good to start with,* he advised the *Make It With Race* audience. *Big bits're always good after. Make sure fire doesn't spread.*

"This power cut's a drag." Hugh Pridham sniffed. "No computer. No games. No TV."

"You get used to it," said Si. "I've been reading books."

"Can you read without moving your lips now?" Denny asked sarcastically.

"I've been planting trees," said Helen. "Collecting stuff like conkers and acorns that's sprouting in the woods? You plant them in the garden and bring them on. Mrs. Ruddock does it. When they're big, you plant 'em back in the woods. Mrs. Ruddock reckons she's planted over three hundred." Helen tossed an oak branch on the fire. "Kind of makes up for trees like this one, you know?"

"It's good." Telly watched the flames. It was very good.

"I've been thinking," said Helen. "Where did Weather Eye come from? I mean, who started it?"

"People like us," said Telly.

"There's another group like us over at Paynter's Cross," put in Grev. "Lorna Turnbull's in it. Know Lorna Turnbull?"

"Why didn't they come up the Edge, then?" sneered Crips.

"How do I know?" Grev shrugged. "Maybe they didn't have the guts. They got the first message. After they saw the comet that night, they started holding meetings, Lorna said."

Telly grew serious. "The point is, the weather's going to change in the future. Everything's going to change. And we're the ones that're going to have to deal with it."

"You know you said something was going to happen?" David Henry looked around. "No kidding—I had this haunted bike."

"Shoulda copped what happened at our house," said Crips darkly. "Somethin' happened all right."

Telly looked thoughtful. "Something happened to everyone."

"Mainly Gary," said Simon.

There was a long and sinking silence. Everything seemed pointless in a world in which life could be suddenly quenched by a freak wave off the Guggles for no good reason at all. Telly searched for the right thing to say. *Don't let them sink,* whispered Lightfoot. *Lift them up. For me.*

Denny wasn't the man to waste a rich vein of hopelessness. He fished out a book from his pocket.

"This is ole Nostradamus, an' what he says is—"

"Nostraddle—who?" Grev ducked to read the title.

"This prophet. He predicted the Great Fire of London, back in, like, fifteen sixty-something? A hundred years before it happened? An' it happened right when he said it would, in sixteen sixty-six."

"Maybe someone read the book," winked Crips.

Denny cleared his throat. "It says here: 'In the year nineteen ninety-nine and seven months, from the sky will come the great King of Terror—'"

"That's gone," said Helen tartly. "The seventh month's July."

"Oh," said Denny, "yeh. Well, anyway, ole Nostradamus says the world's goin' to end in floods an' earthquakes an' stuff any moment. That's what this weather's all about. You know about it, right? You're Weather Eyes. So there's not much point hanging on to things you don't really want. Not if the world's going to end."

Everyone looked at Denny. Telly searched their faces. Denny was playing on their worst fears, seeding hopelessness, killing the spirit of New Weather Eye before it had even been fledged. Denny was horribly dangerous. *Stop him,* whispered Lightfoot. *Stop him now. Or I will.*

"I don't want it to," piped Race. "I don't *want* the world to end."

"Feels like it's going to sometimes," said Hughie.

"I've got thirty quid savings. It better not end before I've blown 'em."

"Blow 'em now, why wait?" said Denny. "No point sitting on it. Might as well let someone else have CDs an' stuff you're tired of. We can spread the cash around up the amusement arcade. If you don't go to town much, I'll get rid of it for you— "

"What are we, stupid?" Telly snatched Denny's book. Ignoring Denny, she cleared her throat. "About Gary. The thing about Gary is . . . it's really hard to talk about, but . . . David knows what I mean."

David Henry nodded slowly. "That bike. Every time I rode it. Gary, all over the place. I gave it up in the end."

"Right. So what I'm trying to *say* is, there's no point being sad about Gary, when all the time he's— "

Denny jumped up. "Book." He snapped his fingers. "Give it back. Now."

"What if Denny's right?" said Hughie Pridham. "S'posing the weather gets worse an' worse? Supposing there's floods and storms and earthquakes an' stuff?"

"Supposing there isn't. Denny's a nerd."

Denny made a lunge for his book. Telly passed it deftly to Crips. Crips jumped up and whacked Denny smartly over the head with it. Denny sat down again quickly. Grev distributed Snak-Size

Chocolate Clubitts, by way of breaking the tension. Race refused his. He fed the fire single-mindedly. He had quite a blaze going now. Telly could see he was worried. She tried to think of a way to lift the mood. It hadn't gone at all the way she'd planned it. Somehow, she'd managed it badly. Everything felt wrong.

Telly looked in the flames. Then she tried again. "You know when you get the Tree in the Meadow? That feeling you get when you're Calming, and everyone else is, too?"

"Get her," said Denny cuttingly. "Teresa Tooth-Brace Saves the World. As if."

Race jumped up. "Take that back, you big fat dingbat drongo."

"What?" A smack on the head with a book, Denny could handle. But garbled Australian insults left him stymied.

"You couldn't never raffle a chook in a pub, you garbage piece of dill." Race had a feeling he had some of it slightly wrong. "Gutless pommie ratbag," he finished weakly. "Dimwit mongrel bludger."

Denny stared. "You're all mad, you are. I'm out of here."

"So go," said Simon Elliot. Then he turned to Telly. "So tell us, what's the plan?"

"Hey, Denny—want to buy a bike?" Crips winked. David Henry grinned. "Twelve-speed Turf Commando, matte black? Forty quid to you."

"Yeah," sneered Denny, "I'd buy a bike off *you*."

"So what's the plan?" asked Si, again. Grev watched Telly for an answer.

Telly shrugged. "What plan?"

"Part Two. The big one. After Calming. And Recruitment."

"There *is* no plan. There's only *us*."

"But you said—you said we'd *do* something."

"We *are* doing something. We're changing things."

"Changing what?"

"Ourselves."

Si and Grev searched Telly's face for the meaning of life, the universe, and everything. *You said we'd do something*. Telly felt cross. All over the world people were rushing around *doing* things. They never stopped. They were doing the world in. *Less doing*, thought Telly. *More being*.

"So you're just the same as before, then?"

"Before what?" asked Si.

"The Edge. The Tree. Everything."

"I'm not," offered Grev.

"Well?" Telly put Si on the spot.

"No," acknowledged Si, "it's different since. I didn't used to like to think about the future, 'cos, like, it's all so depressing? Now I think about it all the time. About what might happen. What I might do in my life. That kind of stuff. It's, like, things can only get better."

Lightfoot stirred. *That's what I'm trying to tell you.*

"That's what I'm trying to tell you." Telly's voice surprised her.

Everything turns out okay in the end.

"Everything turns out okay in the end."

"Not everything," said Denny. "Take a look at this."

Telly and Helen joined Denny at the grizzled lip of the path. Race's head mushroomed between them. They looked where Denny pointed. Half a precipice below, someone's car was bumping down the slope towards Cudlip's Quarry—slowly at first, then gathering speed over hillocks, dipping and rolling and diving, smashing headlong over tracks and mounds and stones and posts and heather-sprung hollows and ditches. They watched it charge an electric fence. It was heading for disaster faster than Telly could think what might have happened.

"I mustn't've put the handbrake on properly. Dad's going to *kill* me."

The moonlight glanced off the hood in the moment it dropped inevitably—really quite satisfyingly—off the edge of Cudlip's Quarry. *Like a rolling stone,* thought Telly. Sure didn't gather much moss on the way down. She guessed Dad wouldn't gather much, either, once he heard. She guessed he'd know who to jump on.

They listened as the whole descent unfolded in spectacular stereo sound. The quarry walls threw back every separate bash and crash, every particular impact, every possible demolition of every possible car part. Telly winced as the roof connected with a ledge on the way down. She didn't have to see it. The sound was so expressive, she could picture it. When the last explosive impact had rolled around and died, and the last hub cap had fallen, ringing, in the rocks, Telly looked at Race.

"Bum-poos," said Race, inadequately.

12

FAST WALKING

 "That does it," said Telly firmly. "I'm going to see Sam Lightfoot."

Helen looked at her. "Why?"

"Because there's something I want to ask him. Because I'm sorting everything out tonight. Because there might not *be* another meeting."

Helen considered the car wreck below. "You can't go now. How?"

"How are we going to get home?" asked Race.

Telly pushed him back. "Keep away from the edge, dumbo."

The lip of the quarry wasn't such a great place to stand. It wasn't such a great place to watch the family car die. Telly watched it burning way below. It looked like the last frame of a car-chase movie. Just before the heroes duck the explosion.

"Watch out," she said, "it might explode."

"It did that already," said Race.

"Good thing you weren't in the trunk," said Helen.

Telly shuddered. "Let's not think about that."

Crips and Si pounded up behind them.

Crips took a long look below. "Wow," he said. "Outstanding."

It was outstanding in a way, supposed Telly. At least it had woken her up. What was she doing standing over a blazing car—*their* car—in the middle of nowhere at one o'clock in the morning, anyway? What had she started? Suddenly she felt tired of it all. It was all too complicated. There were no clear answers to anything, least of all the weather. There was just one thing she had to find out. One thing that *had* to have an answer.

Denny and the others thundered up. Crips grinned. "Like walking, do you, Denny? How far *is* it to Foghanger?"

"Poor you." Grev watched Telly anxiously. "What will you tell your Dad?"

"I'll tell him I was trying to save the world." Telly was close to tears. Sympathy was just what she didn't need. "Then he won't mind a bit."

There was an awkward silence. They watched the burning car split like an orange beneath them.

"We better get going," said David Henry, at last. "We left our wheels down Mount Oak."

Grev nodded. "How will you get back?" he asked Telly.

"We'll walk," said Helen stoutly. "Can't be more'n five miles."

"More like six," said Denny.

"Whatever," said Helen. "Come on."

They skirted the quarry in rambling formation. Race bobbed up at infrequent intervals, equally happy with everyone. He was really glad he'd come. Were all the Weather Eye meetings as slam-bang exciting as this one? No wonder you had to be brave.

At last they reached the cattle grid where Lookout Approach bled rubble and dust on the crossroads. The road ahead shrugged off its moorland bleakness and put on sidewalks and shopfronts as it dipped into Mount Oak. The village lights were comfortingly close. *Quite a few lights,* thought Telly, *for a quarter past one in the morning.* Several winked on as they watched. Northwest over the open moor, the road to Pell Mell stretched coldly away in the darkness.

Si turned to Telly. "So when's the next meeting?"

"There might not *be* another meeting. Leave me alone, why don't you?"

Si stared. "So what do we do next?"

"Think things out for yourself," said Helen sharply.

Grev looked distant. "I know what *I'm* going to do."

"Don't look now," said Crips, "but I think we've done something already."

There was no doubt about it. Mount Oak was waking up. More lights flickered on. Doors banged. Someone shouted something up the street.

Crips grinned. "Must've heard the car crash in the quarry. That'll give 'em something to think about."

"Let's get the bikes and go." David Henry looked nervous. "We don't want any trouble."

"We'll go Back Lane way so we don't get no grief." Crips issued orders easily. Trouble was home ground for him. "We weren't here, okay? We were all home in bed. We don't know nothin' about it."

"Hey, Denny," called Hughie. "Meet me up the video arcade, Saturday?"

"Bring cash," said Denny.

"Can't," said Hughie.

"Why not?"

"Mum keeps my savings book. I got four quid pocket money, though."

"Keep it," said Denny. "Buy yourself a dog. Then there'll be someone who likes you."

"See you around," Crips called to Telly. He watched her, walking backwards, waiting for something—what?

Telly waved. "Take care," she called back, weakly.

Telly and Helen and Denny and Race walked stiffly along the Pell Mell road. Their flashlights picked a lonely path on the tarmac. Denny was whining after half a mile. Curiously, the others didn't pass them. *They must've gone Black House way,* supposed Telly. After a while, she stopped.

"We won't make it home before breakfast at this rate. I'll show you Fast Walking, if you like."

"What's that?" asked Helen guardedly.

"It's this technique. You empty your mind and think of a word, right? Then you think the word over and over and over, and let your legs do the rest. It's really good. Gets you there in no time."

"Me first," said Race. "What's my word?"

Thickhead, thought Telly. "It's *your* word. You have to choose."

Race closed his eyes. "I chose it. It's — "

"Don't! Don't ever tell anyone your word. Okay. Now Helen."

Helen thought. Then she nodded. "I've got one."

"Denny?"

Denny looked scornful. "You're joking."

"Choose a word, Denny," said Helen. "Can't you think of one?"

"Come on," said Telly. "A word you can peg your thoughts on." *I've got a word for you, Denny,* she thought. *How about scumbag, for starters?*

"This is stupid, this is." Denny considered the night-altered landscape ahead. Dark and secret bush shapes watched the road. Sheep blared sudden alarms out of the rubble-strewn blackness. The stars winked coldly overhead. It looked pretty lonely out there, thought Denny. Lonelier still, on your own. "Okay," he said. "I got one."

"One more thing," said Telly. "No talking, all right? Just the word."

"Just the word," said Helen.

Lightfoot led the way. For a long time the word was everything. The night fields brushed past like dreams. No waiting, no walking, no thinking. Nothing but the smoothly bounding word. Telly switched off when at last the crippled old milkchurn stand at the end of Foghanger Lane fitted the pattern in her mind. She breathed a moment deeply, letting the world flood back. Then she turned.

The others stood around her like surprised-looking newly hatched chicks, their cheeks flushed with wild-walking night, their breath steaming slowly in circles, their trembling legs counting the miles.

"Good," said Telly. "Take it slow. Takes a while to get used to it."

"Wow," breathed Denny. "Like, *brilliant*."

"Can we do it some more?" asked Race. "I want to do it again."

"Maybe," said Telly. "Only thing is, if someone interrupts you, you die."

"Oh," said Helen, "is that all?"

Denny shone his flashlight on his watch. "Get this. It's only quarter past two. Six miles over rough ground in just under an hour." He shook his head. "Amazing."

Helen turned. "What's that?"

Telly followed her gaze. Way in the dim southeast,

back the way they'd come, something bright lit the night. Something that blazed like a warning, high on a cone-shaped hill.

"Fire on the Lookout," said Denny. "Car must've flared up or something."

"Can't have," said Helen. "It's right on the top. Like when they used to light the beacon."

"It isn't the car. It's the Wizzen Tree." Telly rounded on Race. "You let the fire spread, you donkey."

"I never lit it," said Race. "Not my stupid meeting."

"Didn't *anyone* stamp the fire out?"

"We all followed you," said Denny.

The faraway glow of the beacon fired the night with newly wakened alarms. No wonder Mount Oak had been stirring. The wind-dried carcass of the Wizzen Tree would have been kindling even as they'd parted. If they hadn't been blinded by the quarry-mouth and a whole mess of niggles and worries, they might, thought Telly, have looked back and seen what they'd done. If they hadn't been Fast Walking all the way home, they might have spotted it earlier. Now it was too late. For the first time in five decades, the Lookout blazed out its warning.

"At least we did something big," said Helen wryly.

Yes, thought Telly, it's big. It's big and it's *all my fault*. She supposed it would burn itself out.

Race yawned a shattering yawn. His six-mile legs knocked together. Telly took his hand. For once, he held her hand meekly. She would have to walk him home down the lane. Get him upstairs in silence. Swear him to secrecy—maybe torture Gonzo a bit. Tuck him up safe and warm in the bush camp in the back bedroom. Telly sighed. The night was slipping away. So many questions, so few answers. The question that needed an answer most would get no airing tonight. Sam Lightfoot would have to wait.

13

SAM LIGHTFOOT

 "Where's the jalopy?" asked Ray. "You take it out down the lane?"

Telly nodded.

"Where'd you leave it? Home Field again?"

Telly nodded again. Nodding was easy.

Ray chuckled. "The demon driver strikes again. Leave it round the front next time you get the urge, will ya?"

They'd all gotten up late, Ray included. He surfaced at half past ten and considered the weather. A steady curtain of rain washed the windows outside. *Good,* thought Telly. The fire on the Lookout had burned in her sleep through every fitful dream. At least the rain would drown it. At 10:45 precisely, every light in the house blinked on.

"Geronimo!" whooped Ray. "Now we're cookin'! Who's for a blow out breakfast?"

Race settled happily in front of the TV. Propping

Gonzo carefully beside him, he channel-hopped for cartoons. The drier banged around in the garage, drying off clothes it had tumbled before it had lost its mind. The dishwasher took up where it had left off five days before. The fridge hummed in the kitchen. Telly listened. The last few days of doom and gloom seemed like a bad dream. The house was waking up. She pounded upstairs. The computer was up, running bulletins ten to the dozen. The Special Conditions was a strange one:

SPECIAL CONDITIONS REPORT

Me mam and her friend's getting off the bus yesterday at Kilkenny Bridge when it starts raining. First they're running home. Then they're looking down and there's tiny baby frogs all over the road. The ground's hopping with them. Mam's friend goes, Kathleen, it's raining frogs, what'll it mean? Mam goes, Means they'll never be believing us. So she brings some home in a bag. Dad goes, Sure, they'll never top that on the network. So I'm telling it so you can try. Clare Devlin, County Cork.

Telly grinned. Her fingers hovered over the keyboard. She could top the Rain of Frogs if she wanted. Stranger by far, was the Tree. Someone else thought so, too:

I am loving Tree Calming, all my friends as
well, now we are doing something we are not so
frightful. It is very strange, even the Piazza
is pin drop at seven o'clock. It is silence
because all the children are in the Tree, even
my bad cousin Tito! We are happy with our
friends in Weather Eye to think maybe not so
much bad things happen in future. Also the
weather is better. Ciao, Nona Arletti,
Florence.

The next two Weather Eyes really had their act
together. Telly was impressed.

Tree-Happy, or what? Not only temps and data-
collecting, but we started Kids for Clean Air.
KCA aims to minimize car use in our neighbour-
hood and save the planet! Two wheels good, four
wheels bad! Complete the following rhyme:
Weather, weather, over the world, kids on your
side,_____? First prize for an excellent rhyme
for "world" is ten KCA bike stickers made of
100% recycled tyres. Watch this space! Dream
on, Preston Novack, Quebec.

▼

Axis 2000—Weather Eyes in Nottingham and sur-
rounding areas! You are invited to the first
official Weather Eye Action Group Meeting at
the Guild Hall, Nottingham, at 10:00, Saturday

1st January 2000. Theme for discussion is: Things to Come—Our Part in a Changing World. Organized by Lita Newhouse, Gemma Bridges, and Martin Buxton, sixth form, Enderby Comprehensive School. Please come. It's Up to Us.

The picture of the Tree in the Meadow flashed up, elbowing Axis 2000 off the screen. Someone had dragged the Tree into a Paintbox program and embellished it, changing its color to brown. They'd added their name, bottom right. Someone else had embellished the embellishments, adding their initials underneath. The Tree looked out, decked in Paintbox icons, its branches making a complicated trellis around the picture. The original message had been long lost under a mess of flowers and doves. Telly smiled. It was good, except—hitting Save and Post, Telly dragged the image into Colorways. Then she optioned Electric Blue on the palette. The Tree flushed from brown to blue. Better. That was one thing they shouldn't mess with, whatever else they did. The Tree in the Meadow was blue, didn't they realize?

Playing now, Telly optioned Morph. A grid with a skeletal Tree blinked up. Telly fixed three separate positions for each of its branches on the grid, clicking on each with the mouse. Then she hit ACT for action. The electric blue Tree waved gently in the wind, its branches changing, or "morphing," from one of three positions to another. Telly watched with satisfaction. She shouldn't make it move, really. The Tree in the Meadow was still. It was just that she couldn't resist it. It seemed so real, somehow. After a while, she Unmorphed. Then she sent the Tree back to the Bulletin Board.

The Privileged Overwrite took her by surprise. It was a message so entirely like her own, she might have written it herself:

STATUS CODE CALMING

PRIVILEGED OVERWRITE

Weather Eyes United! Situation changeable. Outlook, improving. Kids, active on all fronts. Adults, brighter later. Global weather: Fragile, occasional stress, subject to atmospheric influence. Excited? You should be! The twenty-first century is only a weather cycle away! Soon we turn the corner. Earth 2000, One Safe Home in Our Hearts. Something changed already.

Network Southwest: Group Calming at Paynter's Cross, 6:30 for 7:00, Friday 2nd Nov. Be there or be sad. Message ends. YOUR WEATHER EYE.

Telly stared. Your Weather Eye. There was only one Weather Eye, and *she* wasn't about to organize any group Calming at Paynter's Cross. Someone had weaseled in where they shouldn't. Who did they think they were? After two minutes precisely, the Overwrite winked away. Telly's outrage melted. Other messages came and went. Not a whine among them, noted Telly. All were positive, in one way or another. Best of all was the message from Weather Eye Central that flashed out on a Repeat Loop every five minutes or so. Telly glowed as she read it:

Congrats, Global Weather Eyes! Your contribu-
tion in gathering weather information over the
period 1998-9 an enormous boost to overall
picture. Results forwarded to International
Conference on Climatic Change in Sydney,
Australia. Well done, Weather Eyes everywhere!
P.S. Have submitted Seven O'Clock Calming
Initiative as UK entry for the Young Person's
Environmental Awareness Award. Whose baby is
it? Please log in! Best wishes, Weather Eye
Central. One Safe Haven in Our Minds.

Proudly, Telly composed a Loop of her own, giving her code name and number. She named all the others, too. They'd all played a part, after all.

She came downstairs with a warm glow of real satisfaction. Kids could make a difference. Weather Eyes all over the world had proved it.

Race brought Dewie in for lunch. Dewie sat on the kitchen floor between the chair legs, ignoring the lettuce Race thrust under his nose. He ignored his cucumber, as well. Dewie was good at ignoring things. His liquid eyes were blank. He hopped around in a desultory way, rubbing his chin on chair legs, distributing raisins as he went. Race preferred to think of Dewie's droppings as raisins whenever he had to sweep them up, which was every time Dewie got nervous, which was every time Race brought him in. The brightly lit kitchen with its suddenly scraping chair legs made Dewie a positive raisin factory. Race didn't mind too much. Dewie's only other fault was a fondness for electricity cables and the bottoms of people's trousers. Race looked down at him indulgently. Dewie settled into a chicken shape under Ray's legs, munching something or other over his large and impressive ruff. He looked, thought Race, a bit like Henry the Eighth.

"Did you know rabbits eat their own poos?" asked Race, over a cheese and pickle sandwich.

"No kidding." Ray pushed his pickle aside. Didn't look too wonderful, all of a sudden.

"They do, 'cos grass, is like, hard to digest. So sometimes they chew 'em over again."

"Can we change the subject?" Telly looked sternly at Race. "You been snooping on the computer?"

Race shook his head blankly.

"Then how come it was up when the electricity came back on? I never left it running."

"You must've," shrugged Race. "I never."

Guilelessly, Race peeled an orange. He wasn't lying. His memory didn't extend much before the previous day at any given moment. The day the eye of the hurricane had pressed solidly over the fields, the day Ray came—the day the computer Bulletin Board had frightened him out of his wits—were a million miles away in the vague gray everydays behind him. Race had given up worrying. "No worries" was his new motto. He ought, thought Telly, to have a T-shirt printed.

Ray pushed Dewie away from his legs. "Have a heart, mate. If I want my jeans chewed, I'll chew 'em meself." He flipped a cigarette in his mouth. "See this?"

Telly raised an eyebrow. "Where'd you get that?"

"Betty Ruddock. Delivered the old girl's groceries. She says, 'I thought you might be a smoker, like a Woodbine? I've still got my husband's Woodbines in the drawer.' 'You beauty,' I says, and I give her a peck on the cheek. Funny old chook. Thought she was going to stiff out on me. 'Mr. Peters,' she says, 'you are awful.'"

"Mr. Ruddock died," said Telly. "Know what he died of?"

"No, but you're going to tell me."

"Smoking," said Telly. "Like a light?"

Straight after lunch Telly picked up the phone. She dialed the number quickly, counting seconds, giving herself no time to think. If she thought

Sam Lightfoot / 179

about it too much, she wouldn't be able to do it.

At last someone picked up. "Porth Madder 556."

"Sam? It's Telly. Telly Craven. You okay to talk?"

"Sort of. What d'you want?"

"It's just—I didn't know him very well, but—I wanted to say I'm sorry about Gary."

"You should be."

Telly paused. The hard edge to Sam Lightfoot's voice took her by surprise. "We had another meeting last night. Everyone's really sorry about what happened."

"They should be."

"Don't suppose you've been fishing at all since—" Telly floundered. What was she saying? She wished she'd never started. Never called at all. "Don't suppose you feel much like fishing."

"Not much. Did you want something?"

"It's just, David Henry said it wasn't a fishing night. The night Gary—the night, you know, he—"

"It wasn't."

"You don't know why he did it?" How could she ask these things? Insensitive, or what?

"Why he went out in a storm? You should know."

Telly's heart hammered. "What d'you mean?"

Sam Lightfoot paused. Five days' bitterness weighted his voice. "He always wondered why you stopped him from going up the Edge."

Telly's thoughts hurdled back to the Edge. The talk she'd had with Gary. She'd stopped him because she could see he wouldn't live long. Could she have told him that?

"But I told him he ought to be careful. What did he say?"

"Not a lot. He thought you thought he didn't have the guts. He thought he wouldn't be part of it."

"Part of what?"

"The plan."

Telly swallowed. The plan. The stupid, pie-in-the-sky, empty-bottomed plan she'd started for the sake of starting *something*.

Sam Lightfoot went on, words coming easily now. "The night it happened, he goes, 'It's giant waves at Dagmouth. I'm goin' down the harbor, see the yachts. There's yachts slipped their moorings all over.' But *I* reckon he went out on the Guggles instead, jus' to see if he *could*. Jus' all because of *you*."

Lightfoot stirred. *It wasn't my fault. He chose it.*

"It wasn't my fault. He chose it." Telly's voice surprised her.

"Yeh, right. Like, he chose bein' drowned—"

He was watching the storm. He went out too far. It was a spur of the moment thing.

"He was watching the storm," said Telly. "He went out too far. It was a spur of the moment thing."

"Oh," said Sam, "you'd know."

"Yes," said Telly. "I do." *He didn't mean to do it. Be comforted, why won't you?*

"Gary'd never've done it, 'cept for that Weather Eye stuff. You're weird. Get off it, an' don't bother callin' again."

Telly dropped the phone. Holding her stomach, she climbed stiffly upstairs to her room. *Gary'd never've done it. He thought he wouldn't be part of it. He went out on the Guggles. Just to see if he* could. *Gary'd never've. Just all because of* you.

Telly opened her bedroom door. The computer ran messages in the corner, the way it had before lunch, when there'd been everything to shout about. The bulletin board flashed her cheery Loop every five minutes or so. The Loop which claimed her prize. Telly watched it flicker. It seemed to have nothing to do with her. She sat down and wondered who she was. There wasn't much to hang on to. Only a whisper which told her Gary's death wasn't her fault, a whisper she shouldn't be hearing, from a place she didn't want to think about. She remembered the morning the glorious flight of the parrots had flagged the pines with colors, the upside-down, end-of-the-world morning Lightfoot had created himself in his own image. She closed her mind to him now.

There were no prizes for stirring up deep things that ran, for a very good reason, in a channel all their own. So much for making things happen. All there was, was funny, warm, flat, disappointing, wonderful, ordinary everyday life—whatever you chose to make of it. Telly longed to wind back the clock. If only things were back the way they were. Before the storm. Before the accident. Before any of it. She didn't want to be Weather Eye. Only Telly Craven.

Telly Craven sat down at the computer and carefully killed her Loop with a Delete command. If Weather Eye Central hadn't picked up her claim to fame by now, they never would. Telly held her head. Her head thrummed. What had she done? How could she even *think* about claiming some Young Person's Environmental Awareness Award? How about the Getting a Knock on the Head and Messing with Things You Don't Understand Award? She guessed she'd be first up for *that*.

Telly got up. The thrum in her mind deepened. It seemed to fill the house. She wandered onto the landing. The potted plant on the landing windowsill vibrated in its saucer. Fascinated, she watched it. Something was happening. Something big, outside. She started down the stairs, the vibration in the banisters making her hand tingle. The kitchen door beneath her exploded against the wall.

"Dad!" Race streaked through the hall. "It's Dad!"

Telly colored up. Her heart hammered. Dad! Jumping the last four stairs, she reached the front door. Then she ran back to close the kitchen door on Dewie. He'd made a move towards the hall already. He tried to look as though he hadn't.

"Nice try, fluff-for-brains." Telly slammed him in

and rushed off. Dewie blinked stupidly. He didn't know Dad was coming.

Telly closed the front door behind her. The rumble of something big as doom and twice as unstoppable thrilled the air. The walls of the house threw back the sound. Telly felt like bursting. Dad! Returning with the turbine blade like some kind of old-time hero! Riding down the lane in something so tall it could look down on just about everything except the pyramids! Plain, ordinary, homecoming Dad! Just when she needed him most!

14

T H E R E T U R N

Telly jumped up on a granite trough. Race jumped up beside her. Something was coming. Something so big, you couldn't tell it. You had to *be* there. The rumble of the approaching truck traveled through the ground, up through the granite trough, and into Telly's legs. She looked up. The rain had thinned and stopped. The parting clouds showed her enough blue sky to make a whole fleet of sailors' trousers. The sunlight lanced through, lifting the stone from Telly's heart. She could feel it. Everything was going to be all right. A rainbow arched gloriously over the turbines. Once seen, never forgotten. Nothing was clear—or finished. But some things lived in a perfect place, where nothing else could touch them. Telly locked the moment in her less than perfect heart. Then she watched the lane with mounting excitement.

A truck like the side of a house slid, with difficulty,

through the trees. The trees groaned, and let it. The roar of the engine grew throaty. The flashing cab appeared and disappeared. Telly glimpsed the driver, sweating over the wheel.

"He'll go around the side of the house!" roared Ray. "Better get out of the way!"

The mountainous truck broke onto the drive, changing tone, engaging mighty gears. Telly gaped. How long could a truck *be*? Only just long enough. The excitingly white turbine blade it carried took up all the room there was. Race waved and jumped and pointed, yelling soundlessly against the roar of the engine. Telly looked up into the cab. Between the toiling driver and Dad, someone waved and smiled. Someone gloriously familiar, bracing herself, waving madly with her free hand, pointing at Ray, shrieking in disbelief, pushing Dad, covering her face, looking again, shaking her head, laughing, making faces, brushing her hair from her streaming, so-surprised eyes. Telly jumped and shouted she didn't know what. Mum! Mum riding royally home in the cab like Boadicea! Mum, with a smart new coat and a smile like all the triumphant homecomings there ever were rolled into one and made mumlike in one unforgettable moment so long overdue it rushed on Telly like a cloudburst.

Mum. Telly brushed away tears. It seemed so long since she'd seen her—so long in some kind of jagged, alien landscape with no familiar landmarks.

She'd been all right until now. Now she knew what she'd been missing. You didn't know you were thirsty until you saw a well. Telly felt life sweep her up. It swept her into the heart of an ordinary family, through the boisterous reunion half-in, half-out of the truck.

"Race Edwin Peters!" wept Mum. "Pinch me, I'm dreaming!"

Ray pinched her all over. Then he hugged her. They hugged a long time, then they drew back. Ray shook his head and whistled.

"All you need's the hat. You look like the flippin' Queen Mum in that coat. Where'd you get it, a thrift shop?"

"Same place you got those trousers. Walked here from Queensland by themselves, did they?"

Ray grinned. "Just about led the way." He held out the sides of his jeans, stiff with generator grease. "Fair go, Mags. We haven't had a washing machine for almost a week. Been living off bread an' water in a coal hole, haven't we, kids?"

"We made a camp in the back bedroom, we did," gabbled Race, "an' I did driving down the lane, an' Ray rescued Dewie under the shed, *and* we played Squeeze the Monkey. What Squeeze the Monkey is, is first you — "

Ray gagged Race with a hand like a plate. "Weird coupla kids you got here, Mags. Wasn't easy, but I just about straightened 'em out."

Maggie Craven smiled. "Did, did you? Anyone straighten *you* out?"

"Wasn't easy," said Telly, "but I just about stopped him smoking."

Dad joined them, rubbing his hands, with that let's-get-a-crack-on-and-*do*-something look on his face.

"How long's the farm been down?" he asked.

"The turbines? Since yesterday afternoon," said Ray. "Got an ESN around three."

"Hope we get startup clearance soon," worried Dad. "Not much point landing a power supply contract—*if* we get one—if we've got no power to supply."

"Take it easy," said Ray. "It'll all come right. Give a bloke a crack at the fork lift, will ya?"

"The man who backed my car at high speed into the only concrete post on Newquay seafront? *I'll* take the fork lift," said Dad.

Telly grinned. Who wouldn't, who'd heard the story? The photo of Mags 'n' Ray on Newquay seafront wasn't the only memento Ray had left behind him, that last careless summer before he'd emigrated. He'd left Dad a rubbished Sierra to remember him by, as well. Some things never changed, supposed Telly. Ray and her father were just about as different as it was possible to be. Different, but the same. The years had rounded their edges, noticed Telly, watching them work as one and cherishing both. She would always remember the golden afternoon the gleaming white, two-ton turbine blade swung off the truck in its cradle, inch by careful inch; Dad's maneuverings with the fork lift; Ray's shouted directions; Tony the driver's helpful jokes; Race's not-so-helpful suggestions; Mum's warm arm around her. The muddle in the back of her mind seemed suddenly a part of someone else. A part of Weather Eye. Whoever *she* was.

Mum squeezed Telly's arm. "Come on, let's leave them to it."

Arm in arm, they walked back up to the house. "Like the new coat," said Telly. "Where'd you get the pin?"

"This?" Mum looked down at the pin on her lapel. An electric blue Tree spread its arms against a green ground, its interlaced branches forming the words *Calm Earth*. "A bunch of kids were selling them outside the store in Cardiff where I got my coat. Some environmental group, they started it up themselves. We had quite a chat. They were saying they think the pace of life's too fast. Not enough time to think what we're doing. I think they've got a point." She fumbled in her pocket. "Here. I got you one."

Telly caught it. "Thanks." She turned it over in her hand. Nice pin. The Tree had taken root just about everywhere, it seemed. "Did they like the presentation in Wales? Think we got a contract?"

"Fingers crossed," said Mum. "Went down quite well at Wessex Power as well, but you never can tell with these people. Should know soon, one way or the other. How've things been while I've been away?"

"Okay. I had a bit of an accident."

Mum looked at her. "Dad told me. A bump on the head, wasn't it? All right now, I hope?"

Telly squeezed her mother's arm. "All right now *you're* back."

"Can't've been much fun with the power off."

"Not fun. But quite—exciting."

"Exciting? Around here? What've I been missing?"

Telly swallowed. Quite a lot, she thought. Recent events were converging like some fateful hidden iceberg she was bound to collide with, sooner or later. So much had happened under the surface. How much would stick out on top?

The tip of the iceberg showed itself unmistakably on Roundup Southwest while the casserole was browning in the oven. Dad and Ray blustered in, talking cranes and hoists and likely blade-installation days over the kitchen TV. Telly snuck close to the set. She'd have turned Roundup Southwest over or off, except Dad always watched the news. Second up was an item about the fire on the Lookout. Telly looked around anxiously. Mum was clattering dishes. Race was under the table talking to himself over a precarious pile of placemats. Dad was busy washing up with Ray. It might—just might—be all right.

"Dropped the pickup back to Will Fishbone on the way," Dad was saying. "Denny helped me back it into the yard. Funny, that. He's usually about as helpful as a stone."

Ray grinned. "Hear you had the car stolen."

"Darndest thing." Dad toweled his hands by the sink. "Probably joyriders. Nowhere's safe these days. Move back, will you, Telly? I can't see through your head."

Telly reluctantly moved away from the television. At least she'd obscured the fire on the Lookout. Some old trout from the council was wrapping it up with a few small crumbs of comfort:

"Funny thing is, whoever set the fire did us a favor. Burned off all that rubbish. It's been quite something to see the beacon blazing after all these years. I think we can see it as a warning. I think we all realize we've got a lot of things wrong, environmentally speaking. The council will be inviting local schoolchildren to plant a young oak on the Lookout on January the first to mark the beginning of a new millennium, and a new beginning in the parish."

"That's nice, isn't it?" said Mum vaguely. "Race? Give me a hand with the table?"

A burned-out car wreck flashed on the screen. "What about last night's car vandalism?" asked the interviewer.

Race looked up. His eyes connected with Telly's.

"Where are you sitting, Dad?" asked Telly desperately, pushing past him, scraping chairs.

"Where I always sit." Dad shushed her with his hand.

The camera panned back from Cudlip's quarry. The council spokesperson filled the screen in front of it. "The council will, of course, be taking measures to prevent further acts of vandalism of this kind . . ."

"Dumping cars in the quarry," said Mum. "It's too bad. Whoever did it wants a kick up the bum."

Might as well give me mine now, thought Telly. She looked over miserably at Ray.

Ray winked. "Shall we tell the old man now? Put him out of his misery?"

Telly looked away.

"Hey. He has to know sometime. Doesn't he?"

Dad looked from Ray to Telly. "He has to know *what* sometime?"

"It's like this." Ray steered Dad into a chair. "The car isn't stolen at all, mate."

Dad stared. "It isn't?"

"Kids've got the car. Had it all along." Ray enjoyed his moment. "Joke's on you, mate. Stolen. I just about bust a gut laughing. Where'd you get off lettin' a coupla kids pull the wool over your eyes like that?"

"Where in God's name is it?"

"Parked up in Home Field."

"No, it isn't," said Telly.

Pat Craven looked from one to the other. "Perhaps *someone* would care to tell me where the car is? Or shall we pretend we don't know?"

"I know where it is, Dad," offered Race.

"No, he doesn't," Telly said quickly.

"Where is it, then?"

Race jumped up. "It's *there.*"

The council spokesperson on Roundup Southwest had moved on to talk about reforestation: "Schemes of this sort will counter vandalism by offering useful employment . . ." Meticulously, Race indicated the spot onscreen—the *exact* spot—where the family car smouldered in the background.

"Hang on a minute." Mum put down the veggies. "You're telling me that's *our* car?"

Dad rounded furiously on Telly. "What the devil's going on?"

Ray grinned. "Looks like they made monkeys out of all of us. What *I'd* like to know is how the flamin' heck they — "

"I still don't see how it's *our* car."

"I *knew* there was something fishy about it. You took it from the hospital parking lot, didn't you?"

"Hospital?" Mum looked at Dad. "What hospital? Has Telly been in the hospital?"

"*Didn't* you?"

Telly held her head. "My head hurts. I don't feel well. I've not been well all along."

Dad opened his mouth. Then he closed it again.

The Return / 193

"It's my fault." He looked at Mum. "Behavioral changes, the doctor said. I should've taken her back."

They all looked at Telly as though she'd grown an extra arm. Behind their heads Roundup Southwest featured the funeral of local boy Gary Lightfoot. Dressed in black, Sam Lightfoot looked palely out at Telly. Telly looked back, summoning up all the composure she had left plus quite a lot she hadn't, blanking out everything but Sam's pale face and the paler clock on the wall.

"It's seven o'clock. I think we should all sit down." Telly sat down at the table. One by one, they joined her. No one said anything at all. Telly closed her eyes. "Now we do this. And think Calm."

Breathing deeply, she emptied her heart and mind. Nothing happened at first. TV weatherman Russell Gammy followed the news with the weather: "A generally brighter outlook, with that troublesome front we've been experiencing over the last few days lifting now over the continent . . ." Telly pictured it lifting. She pictured the sun coming out, all over the bruised-looking world. Through the shafting sunlight winked the Tree. Telly ran to it, gladly. Then she stopped. It wasn't time, she knew. Hand in hand with Lightfoot, she walked the lovely meadow for the very last time but one. Parting, Lightfoot turned. Telly smiled. *I know. Go on, go on, go on.* She watched him cross the meadow. She watched him meld with the Tree. Together, they were perfect. *Goodbye,*

Lightfoot, she thought. The Tree blazed. Telly fell. Then she opened her eyes.

Marvelously peaceful, she looked around the table. They all had their eyes closed but Race. Quietly Race poured salt and pepper together into an interesting heap.

Ray opened his eyes. Then Dad. Last of all, Mum blinked open.

"Phew," said Dad, "that's better. Feels like a ton weight's gone."

Mum rubbed her eyes. "Those kids I met. The ones who sold me the pins. They said *they* stopped whatever they were doing at seven o'clock and all thought calm things together. It's really rather good. I was thinking about a tree; what were you thinking about?"

"Tucker," said Ray. "Let's eat."

Later that night in bed, when all the wrangling and the explanations were done, and she couldn't explain it all any more than she'd tried to already, Telly heard them talking. The burble downstairs rose and fell with her hopes. It wouldn't be too bad, she knew. Hadn't Mum said it was only a car? Insured, after all? Weren't there more important things to worry about? Dad supposed there were. He supposed they should just be grateful she hadn't killed herself—or anyone else. Driving around like that. It didn't bear thinking about. He supposed an appointment with the clinical psychologist mightn't be a bad idea. Telly held her breath. She's fine, said Mum, I know she is. Time would tell. But she had a really strong feeling things would turn out fine.

Telly closed her Weather Eye Wallet. Then she turned out her light. Lightfoot's farewell had left her peaceful, more peaceful than she'd ever felt before in her life. Everyone's days tumbled on, around and around like the wheeling blades of the turbines, around and around and on and on and on. Until they didn't. And that was all right, too.

Fear of storms had gone. The burden of being Weather Eye had gone. Lightfoot had gone. The Tree had gone—till the last time. Race was unworried. Even the Drafts had gone. What about the weather? Telly listened. Then she turned over and went to sleep. The night was still. It wasn't her concern.

15

THE DAY THE

CRANE CAME

Greville Jackett walked crisply up the path. He tweaked a neatly folded *Western Morning Herald* out of his sling as he approached the Craven's front door. His canvas sling was freshly charged with all the news that mattered. The last few days had brought about a full resumption of his duties. He had "Business As Usual" written all over him, thought Telly. Almost as usual, at least. There was an extra spring in his step, perhaps. And an extra paper in his hand. He offered it to her, grinning. He looked pretty full of himself.

"What's all this, then?" asked Telly.

"Me 'n' Si did it. Read it an' see."

Telly read:

THE COMET
Twenty-first Century News for shakers and movers everywhere! Letters, Comps, Real Ideas!

Weather Eye Updates! Action Group Meetings!
Local Sports Rundown! Gary Lives!—first issue
dedicated to Gary Lightfoot, by permission G & M
Lightfoot, Crow's Nest, Porth Madder.

Computer-printed on bright blue paper, *The Comet* was certainly eye-catching. So was its bold-font headline: "END OF THE WORLD—NOT! WEATHER EYES MAKE THE DIFFERENCE—OFFICIAL!"

Weather Eye Central's announcement about the contribution made by amateur weather-watchers to the Climatic Change Conference in Sydney, Australia, had been reprinted underneath. The article ran on to talk about the way local Weather Eyes sent in information; how global information had revealed the big picture; how the big picture showed, for the first time, signs of a change in the air. The style was bright and lively. Telly was impressed.

"Wow. When d'you think of this?"

"After the Lookout. I started thinking about Gary. Then I knew what to do."

Telly nodded slowly. She smiled at Grev over the paper. "Weekly or monthly?"

"Whenever we got enough news. Only good news, see? David Henry's in it. He wants to come over an' do an interview, we're doin' windfarms next issue, stuff about if we got windfarms it's good because —"

"Because windfarms don't burn fossil fuels to make

electricity. Because they don't make global warming worse. Because renewables make a difference."

"Right. Stuff like that." Grev looked wicked. "What did the no-brain farmer run his wind turbines off?"

"I don't know, what?"

"Electricity."

"Ha," said Telly, "ha."

"Anyway. David Henry's doin' environmental stuff, I'm doin' local news. Si's doin' sports an' competitions. An' we're having Bikes for Sale an' Fishing Tips an' Calming times and everything good someone does. An' it's —"

"Brilliant," said Telly, reading it. "It's so—positive. Makes you feel you can *do* something. What's this at the bottom mean?"

Grev looked. "Denny put that in. Dunno what it means."

Telly read out the strange-looking verse:

The walls will change from brick to marble, seventy-five
*   peaceful years.*
Joy to humankind, the aqueduct reopened.
Health, abundant fruit, joy and mellifluous times.

She looked up. "Sounds hopeful, anyway."

"Nostraddlemus," said Grev.

Telly folded the paper. "It's really nice you dedicated it to Gary. I think he'd've liked it a lot."

Grev looked down, well-pleased. Then he looked out across the field. "See you got the new blade ready."

Telly nodded. "Installing it today. It's going to be rough—'specially for Uncle Ray."

Grev considered the newly minted blade waiting under its turbine. The remains of the damaged blade had been stripped away in preparation. The unbalanced, two-bladed spinner awaited its brand-new tooth.

"Why's it going to be rough?"

"Ray's going up on the spinner. Dad doesn't want him to."

"Why's he doing it, then?"

"Someone's got to screw up the bolts. Ray did the accounts. He says we can't afford to hire a second crane. Dad wanted two cranes—one to lift the blade in place, one to lift a man-basket so's someone can stand in it and screw up the bolts on the spinner. But Ray says he'll do it without. Ray's going to climb through the cabin roof and sit on the spinner, save hiring another crane."

Grev looked up at the turbine. "Rather him than me."

"That's what Dad said," said Telly. "And we've got Startup tomorrow. And what I wondered is —"

"I thought they shut you down."

"Electric Southwest?" Telly nodded. "They did. They rang Dad up last night. We've got Startup

Clearance from twelve o'clock tomorrow. And we're starting first."

"How'd you mean, first?"

"Everyone starts up tomorrow. Every windfarm in the area's got clearance now they fixed the power lines. If we all start up together there'll be a power surge. Has to be staggered, else we'll swamp the grid—or blow the substation—so they asked us to start up one by one. And we're the most westerly, so we're starting first."

"Smart," breathed Grev. "It's, like, *you're* starting *everyone*."

"Right. And what I wondered is, can you ask—"

"Like, when Crossways sees your turbines goin', they'll start up theirs, then Caldicott'll start, then when Windy Ridge sees Caldicott *they'll* start. Then, like, *all* the windfarms'll start turnin', all over the whole—"

"So can you ask Crips to bring them?"

Grev sobered. "Bring who?"

"Everyone. To the Startup. Mum says baked potatoes, maybe soup in a cup. I'm doing hot dogs, Race is making popcorn. Around twelve o'clock tomorrow. So can you ask Crips to round 'em up?"

"Round 'em up. Crips." Grev nodded. "I got Slaughter Mill next on my round. When you say everyone—Hughie? And Denny?"

"Everyone," said Telly.

Everything was turning out a million times better

than expected. Just three things bothered Telly. One: the car. Mum and Dad had been incredibly under-standing—almost *too* understanding—but she still felt bad about it. Two: The third Weather Eye mes-sage—who'd posted it? Just who was Weather Eye now? Three: What else? Sam Lightfoot.

"Pass me the number three," hissed Ray. "These bolts is mighty big."

Telly looked up at Ray through the hatch in the roof of the cabin. She fumbled the no. 3 wrench and passed it up to him as quickly as she could.

Ray grasped it. "Thanks, mate."

Telly watched him straighten, thirty-two meters high, on the wind-chilled top of the turbine. The wind vane buzzed beside the open hatch. There were no safety nets, no grips, no clamps, no lad-ders—nothing but a nylon rope snaking back down the hatch, securing Ray to the machine bed. It'd probably kill him if he fell, despite his safety harness, Telly knew. Ray was out there with nothing but guts behind him. Telly watched his legs. She couldn't see his expression. His face, dark against the wide blue sky behind him, gave no clues at all.

She wished he wouldn't do it. Mum wished he wouldn't. Dad, way down at the base of the turbine, at the controls of a red-necked crane the size of a cliff, wished he wouldn't. They'd taken some persuading. Especially when she'd insisted on going up to help him. He'd need help, wouldn't he? Well, yes, said Dad, he would. He supposed it would be all right if Telly followed Ray up to the cabin and passed him out tools. *If* she stayed well away from the hatch when he lowered the blade in place.

Everything was in place. Everything except Ray. He disappeared from the mouth of the hatch. Telly heard cautious footfalls above her. One step, two steps, three. That would be about it. Ray had around twelve square meters of walking room up on the roof of the cabin, calculated Telly. Sounded like quite a lot, but it wasn't. He would have to catch the end of the blade as Dad lowered it in its sling, inch by cautious inch. Guide the end of the blade into its hub in the central spinner. Straddle the spinner. Slot in the bolts and do them up. Twenty bolts. Ray had the bolts in a leather pouch at his waist.

Telly climbed up on the gearbox and stuck her head out the hatch. She had no intention of staying well back and missing all the excitement. The air was heady up among the turbines. On a level with the other turbine cabins, Telly took in the view. Beyond the marching pylons that didn't dwarf her anymore, the moor rolled away to the wide, gray, indistinct horizon. Foghanger looked toylike, the Crossways turbines ridiculously close. On the northern coastline beyond them gleamed the sea. Telly snapped out of it. This was no time to be admiring the view. Ahead of her, Ray crouched behind the spinner. Dangling dizzily not ten meters above him, the startlingly white fifteen-meter-long blade hung in the sky, carefully poised in its sling. Telly looked down. A safe distance away below her, Race and Mrs. Ruddock looked like dolls in a bowling alley. Mum stood closer, waiting.

"Okay!" Ray waved his arms. "Okay! Lower away!"

Mum waved her arms, confirming the signal to Dad in the crane cabin. The jib, or crane neck, lurched as Dad engaged the controls. The hanging blade nodded, turning very slightly. Nothing seemed to happen at first. The crane roared, Ray waited, the sunlight flashed off the blade—such a big blade, thought Telly. Such a very big, brutal, crushing, two-ton weight of fiberglass. Such a very small, easily hurt, flesh-and-blood uncle underneath.

Telly narrowed her eyes, watching her uncle's back, desperately trying to see how many long hot summers Ray had left on his tab. No fateful dates or numbers rose to fill her mind. Would Ray croak on some distant coral beach with a happy smile and a six-pack in his hand? Or hanging off a turbine, like a fish on a string? It wasn't hers to know. Had it ever been, really? Telly swallowed. Anything! Could happen!

There was no doubt about it. The blade was coming down. The complicated tendons in the jib screeched and complained as it dropped the blade minisculely lower. *Dad must be sweating,* thought

Telly. *It must be like pickup sticks, only worse. The sort of game where you killed someone if you blew it.* Closer, slowly—and closer. Ray reached out. He flailed, steadied, cursed. Why wouldn't he wait? Telly held her breath. It *would* be Ray up there against the wide blue sky, free as a tumbling spaceman on a line and twenty times as reckless. No one else would be stupid enough.

The blade shivered, dropping five centimeters—ten. Ray reached, and had it. Telly tensed. She checked first base on the ground. Mum made "lower gently" gestures to Dad. Ray consolidated his grip. Telly hoped he was prepared to let go again if the blade swung away; one false move would fetch him off the cabin. The crane roared, inclining its neck towards the spinner. Centimeter by centimeter—ever so gently—Dad slowly eased the sling down. Ray lined up the end of the blade with its waiting hub in the spinner, glancing from one to the other—hub, end, end, hub. The distance narrowed. Ray crouched, watching his fingers, making final adjustments. Almost—almost—*in!* The big-business clunk of the blade in its bearing vibrated throughout the cabin. Telly checked Mum, making violent "cut it" gestures to Dad. The crane changed its tone as Dad applied the brake. Ray slipped down onto the spinner, a leg on either side of the blade. He fumbled behind him for the wrench. Glancing back at Telly, he brought out a single bolt.

"All right?" she called.

"No worries." But his face was awfully white.

Ray's back and shoulders twisted as he worked the bolt with the wrench. He finished and brought out another. Telly watched intently. One down, nineteen to go. The bolts on the outside edge of the hub would be the tricky ones. Ray worked steadily for a long time, fishing finger-size bolts out of his pouch at regular intervals, working his way around one side of the blade, then the other. He kept his mind on the job, noted Telly. Ray never seemed to look down. Resting his head against the side of the blade, he slipped in the bolts on its outer edge, fumbling washers on with difficulty. Telly longed to help him, but Ray moved smoothly on, leaning out, hugging the blade with one arm, tightening bolts with sweeping wrench movements with the other. He seemed to be all right. Then suddenly he wasn't. Something dropped heavily and rattled away off the spinner.

Ray looked down. "Can you believe that? I only dropped the last bolt."

"You've got another one, haven't you?"

"No," said Ray, still looking down. "But you have. Back in the cabin."

Scrambling down off her perch on the gearbox, Telly searched the cabin with desperate, not-seeing eyes. Bolts, bolts, bolts. Every moment Ray was out there on the spinner was a moment when anything could happen. Bolts? There they were. Right under her nose, in an open box on the generator. Telly grabbed two and spun back around to the hatch. Climbing up, she fed them out to Ray across the bird-streaked cabin roof.

"Here. Ray." She clunked the bolts to show him. "Ray. I brought you two."

But Ray didn't turn around and take them. Instead, he leaned against the turbine blade. Telly looked down, but the others couldn't see it—Ray, looked tired and defeated, and not as young as he once was. Not as nerveless, either.

"Ray. Are you all right?"

Ray didn't move. He didn't respond for a minute. "I got the shakes. I'm done, Telly. You're uncle's weak as water."

"Me, too." Telly pulled in Ray's safety line, keeping her voice dead level. "*And* I just got all grease on my hands off the generator. I hate that. Have I got grease on my face?"

Ray mumbled something about never looking down or you were dead. Telly dropped a loop of his safety line neatly over the gearbox below her. That should take up some slack.

"Ray. Have I got dirt on my face? Are you going to tell me, or what?"

Ray spun around testily. "I'm stuck up on a greasy pole like a monkey, and you're worried about — "

"This bolt. Take it. The wrench is behind you. Mind you don't drop it this time."

The Day the Crane Came / 207

"That'd be right. I'm only the dill who's done up all the others without dropping 'em. Like to come up and do better? Whenever you've adjusted your face?"

Ray snatched the bolt. He jammed on a washer. Slotted the bolt in. Grabbed the wrench. Testily tightened it up. He gathered himself and stood, releasing the sling from the blade in a grand gesture. The sling fell away. Mum signaled to Dad. Dad revved the crane. The jib nodded slowly away from the spinner. Mum jumped and waved. Race went silently bonkers, way down below with Mrs. Ruddock. Ray unstrapped his leather bag and handed it down to Telly. Telly gripped his hand. She wasn't about to let go. Ray looked back. The blade was safely bolted in, all twenty bolts in place. It wasn't about to go anywhere in a hurry. Ray swung his weary legs into the hatch. Neither was he, after this.

Telly noticed how shaky he was on the long climb back down the tower. Jumping lightly off the ladder way ahead of him, she watched Ray climbing down. Ray descended slowly, searching for rungs with his feet. Telly waited. Uncle Ray. He'd been throwing good humor around like he had an endless supply, all the last few stormy, tightly packed, sharp-edged, thoroughly peculiar days. How would she ever do without him?

Ray found bottom at last. He looked at Telly uncertainly. He'd been afraid all along, realized Telly.

But he'd gone out on the spinner just the same. Telly felt like hugging him. Suddenly she did. It was a long, warm, melting kind of hug.

"Nasty moment back there," Ray said at last.

Telly nodded. "Thought I was going to have to shout at you."

"Did, didn't you?" Ray grinned, looking down.

Telly waited. "Ready?"

"Ready."

Telly opened the cubicle door. They stepped out into the sunshine.

16

S T A R T U P

Race turned up the heat under his pan. He glanced at the kitchen clock. Five minutes to make it. Two to toss it in syrup and butter. Five minutes to hustle it down the field in time for Startup. Popcorn didn't take long.

Race examined his tray. Great big bowl to tip it in. Paper cups to serve it. Pile of paper napkins for sticky mouths and fingers. Mum had melted his syrup and butter. He only had to pop the corn and toss it. The others had streamed off outside and left him to it. What, after all, could go wrong?

Race listened carefully. Nothing yet. Once the first few had exploded, the rest of the hard maize bullets in the tightly lidded pan would burst into a surprising volume of fragrant, soft popcorn in seconds. All he had to do was watch the pan. And listen. Once the pinging inside it started, he would whip the pan off the heat. Had he put too much corn in? Too late to look now. He'd been caught that way before. The minute you took the lid off to see how the popcorn was going on, it exploded all over you. *Keep lid on till popcorn pops,* he advised the *Make It With Race* millions. *Never look in till it's finished.*

The phone rang annoyingly in the hall. Race shimmied his pan on the electric ring, adjusting the heat down a little. *Mind you don't burn it,* he told his audience. *You got to wait till it's ready.* The phone in the hall rang on and on and on. *Keep popcorn moving,* advised Race. *Else it goes all of a sudden. Mind you don't*—oh, bums to it. Smacking down his wooden spoon, Race ran to pick up the phone.

"Pell Mell 839? Hello? Um, not really, no. Everyone's out down the field." Race listened. Noises from the kitchen. "Race Craven—I will, yeah." Race dragged the phone lead to its furthest extent. He could hardly hear what the woman on the other end was saying. Why wouldn't she hurry up and go? Couldn't she *tell* he was busy? "Yeah . . . yeah." Race covered the receiver and listened. Something was happening in the kitchen. Something pretty drastic. Panic rose in his chest. "I'll tell her. Right. We do, yes." Why wouldn't she hurry up and finish? Stupid phone call. Stupid popcorn. "I will. Okay. Got to go now, bye." Slamming down the phone Race burst through the kitchen door.

Quite a lot had happened in the kitchen while

he'd been gone. First a firing squad had shot the lid off the pan on the cooker. Then they'd sandblasted popcorn all over the ceiling. Then it had snowed popcorn. Race looked with horror at the kitchen. Popcorn all over the cooker, popcorn all over the work surfaces. Popcorn all over the table, the breadboard, the cupboards. Popcorn in the sink. He lifted his foot. Popcorn all over the floor. It was unbelievable how much popcorn there was. Race filled the smoking pan with water. The pan hissed. He found the lid behind the cooker. Then he bent wearily to his task. *Pick up bits,* he advised his audience. *Especially bits in floormat. Else Mum kills you. True.*

Beyond the corn-white kitchen, beyond the house, the trellis, the veggie garden and the clotheslines, a small crowd milled around the hot dogs. Down among the turbines the countdown to Startup was well under way. A brisk breeze lifted the cloth on the table under the newly repaired turbine where Mum dispensed baked potatoes. Might as well make a bit of a thing of it, Mum said. How about inviting a few friends? It made a good excuse for a get-together after the storm, didn't Telly think?

Telly did think. She looked around. The scene looked small and faraway through the wrong end of Dad's binoculars. Telly turned them the right way around and everything jumped out at her. Ray turning sausages on the barbecue; the food-and-drink-loaded table; the rockets in milk bottles lining the ridge beyond it—rockets filched from Race's stash; the waiting turbines beyond *that*, with the wind-licked moor behind them; the Gileses chatting with the Fishbones; the friendly faces everywhere, glad for any excuse for a celebration after the wind-battered gloom and tension of the last extraordinary two weeks. Crips had excelled himself. Everyone was there. Grev. Si. Hughie. Hughie's sister, Caroline. Denny, oddly sociable, hamming Fast Walking, like he was funny or something, whenever he caught Telly's eye. David Henry, cub reporter, anxious to capture the event for *The Comet*. Helen Fishbone and Helen Fishbone's best friend, dorky Kayleigh Mason. Even Sam Lightfoot. Telly's heart jumped. Sam Lightfoot, eating a cheesie baked potato by the hedge with Lorna Turnbull. And the rest of the Paynter's Cross crowd.

"Won't be long now." Dad rubbed his hands. "Just gone quarter to twelve. Don't wander off, now, will you?"

"Would I?" Telly drank her soup. She was only the single most important person there. Only the person with their finger on the button. In less than fifteen minutes she would key in the single computer command which would trigger every wind turbine in southwest England. The command would go out from the computer in the base of the newly repaired turbine. It would instruct each of the other South Hill turbines to check all systems and start when they were ready. Way over the moor, eager for Startup themselves, Mr. and Mrs. Gunner of Crossways Windpark waited to see the South Hill turbines in action before they triggered their own. Beyond Crossways, Caldicott was on stand-by—the third in the long chain of windfarms which waited on Telly's command. It was only right she should start the first turbine, said Dad, when she'd had such a rotten time with the blessed thing. Might put things back in perspective. Telly had nodded. It might.

It would be a big moment. A moment that would set things right again, back the way they were before the turbine blade had ever fallen off; a moment which would bring everything full circle. Telly planned to enjoy it. She might've been able to, if she hadn't spotted Sam Lightfoot. Would he—did he—still blame her?

"Where's Race with that popcorn?" wondered Dad. "I like a bit of homemade popcorn."

"Be out in a minute," said Telly. "He only had to pop it."

Dad wandered off. He couldn't keep still if he tried. Telly watched him scolding Ray for teasing Mrs. Ruddock. Mrs. Ruddock looked pink as a shrimp, sandwiched between the two of them. Mum joined them with glasses of cider, teasing Ray for teasing Mrs. Ruddock. Everyone laughed and swayed, especially Mrs. Ruddock. Ray put his arm around her. Mrs. Ruddock grew pinker. Telly watched them sadly. The knowledge that Ray was going home to Australia after Christmas colored his every move. His every joke was the funniest ever to Telly, his laid-back smile, the warmest and best in the world. Dad wandered restlessly back. Slipping inside the turbine tower he paged Systems Checklist on the computer, making the turbine that would trigger all the others run a health check on itself for the millionth time that morning.

Telly saw Crips heading her way with a hot dog in his hand and the irritatingly meaningful look he wore lately whenever he was near her—as though they shared some kind of secret, thought Telly. The only secret she was likely to share with Crips was what a moron he was—and that was no secret. Suddenly smitten with guilt, Telly moved away before he reached her. Hadn't he done what she'd asked him to? Again? Hadn't he been her trusty lieutenant? Was it his fault he liked bombing people with Coke cans out of school bus windows and popping animals with air rifles on weekends? Well, actually it was. It wasn't anyone else's. Crips 4 Telly. *In your dreams,* thought Telly.

Sam Lightfoot turned when Telly trod on him.

"Hi, Telly," he said. "All right?"

Telly swallowed. "Fine."

"Baked potatoes to *die* for. I've had two. With cheese."

Telly smiled uncertainly. "I'm waiting for homemade popcorn."

Sam nodded. "Nice. Nice the windfarm's starting up. Get things back to normal."

"Right," said Telly, not at all normal herself. What would he find to say next? Something to bring her reconstructed world crashing down around her ears? Just when everything had settled down at last?

"Gary liked popcorn," said Sam casually. "Me an' him had stacks in the movies. The way he used to eat it, he'd grab this, like, *ginormous* handful, stuff it in, half of it went on the floor. Stupid way to eat it. He always done it that way, every time."

Gary. Telly listened nervously. *Here it comes,* she thought.

Sam wiped his mouth. "Saw 'im the other afternoon."

"Saw who?"

"Gary. The afternoon you rang me. I saw him on the stairs. Really weird. I was going up the stairs and he, like, walked right through me."

Telly stared. "He did?"

"After Gary walked through me, I kind of felt different, you know?"

"Yes," said Telly. "I know. I saw him, too. Sort of."

Sam Lightfoot looked at Telly. "It's all right, isn't it? I mean—everything turns out okay in the end—doesn't it?"

"You're almost there." Telly smiled. "Makes a difference, doesn't it?"

Sam nodded. "Makes a difference to me."

Telly circulated a bit, avoiding Crips. Time was ticking on. She wandered back to the table under the turbine. Race was arguing with Mum. He had popcorn stuck up the back of his tracksuit. Quite a bit in his hair.

". . . and I *am* if I want to."

"I think not," said Mum.

"Ray said I could."

"Ray can say what he likes."

"I can if I want to. I stuck 'em in the bottles. I can —"

"Stick *you* in a bottle in a minute. You're not lighting the fireworks and that's that."

"Where's this popcorn, then?" asked Telly.

"Up your jumper," sulked Race.

Mum showed her the popcorn bowl. "I wouldn't, if I were you."

Telly looked in disparagingly. "Bit fluffy, isn't it? What did you do, kick it around the kitchen?"

"Stupid popcorn," said Race. "Stupid cowbrain phone call."

"What phone call?" said Mum.

Race shrugged. "Someone rang about whales."

"Whales?" Mum looked puzzled. "What did they say?"

"There's a contact thingie in the post. About powerful whales or something."

"Power for Wales, you dimbo," said Telly.

"Must be Welsh Power." Mum stared.

"It's a contract!" Telly colored up. "You did it! A contract in the post!"

"How long for?" asked Mum. "Did they say?"

Race thought. "Inishly one. Extended something for two."

"Initially one year, an extended option for two." A slow smile spread over Mum's face. "That's a twenty-four-month contract, probably renewable after *that*, once we get a foot in the door—Pat! Did you hear what Race just—"

"That's great." Pat Craven smiled by the turbine door. He shook his head admiringly. "That's just great," he said.

Race brightened. "We got a contrac', we got a contrac', we got a con—"

The family discussion that followed rolled along on a swell of mounting excitement. Might they visit Australia? Race jumped in. They might, perhaps, said Mum. Good on you, Mags, said Ray. Drop me a line when you're coming. The barbie scrubs up pretty good. And a new car? put in Race. Went without saying, said Dad. Did it? said Mum. How about new bikes all around? Dad frowned. No car? What about the shopping? There's a bus, said Mum. We'll manage. Someone's got to do something to help the environment. Dad looked up at the turbines. I don't know, he said. We're doing more than most. How about a motorbike? said

Mum. Remember that old BSA you used to take me out on? Dad smiled and nodded. How could I forget?

Helen found Telly in the turbine tower. The twin computers flickered. Three minutes to Startup and counting, said the digital clock onscreen. Helen closed the cubicle door behind her. The glowing Startup Checklist lit Telly's face and hands.

"Not long now," said Helen.

"Should call the others," said Telly. "They've almost forgotten, they're so wound up about that contract."

"Brilliant news," said Helen. Telly watched the screens. Helen cleared her throat. "School next week, worse luck. Coming to the meeting at Paynter's Cross on Friday? Party after at Lorna's."

"I don't know," said Telly. "I'm not Weather Eye anymore."

"No," said Helen. "I am."

"You sent the third message?" Telly stared.

Helen grinned. "And I'm going up to Nottingham for Axis 2000. That Weather Eye Action Group Meeting? And I nominated you for the Environmental Awareness Award. For Calming. And all the rest."

Telly swallowed. "Calming's not mine anymore."

"No," said Helen, "it's everyone's. But it was you that started it all."

"I tried to make something happen, but I never

thought—" Telly grinned. "Now it's spreading all over the place."

"Why don't you come up to Axis 2000? It's going to be a really big meeting. Tell them all how you started it."

"Maybe I will." Telly cleared the computer screens and initiated Startup Sequence. Then she looked up. "I'm glad it's you."

"Glad it's me what?"

"Weather Eye."

Helen looked down. "I only did it because you said there might not be any more meetings. I thought you could do with a hand."

Telly nodded. "I did."

"You're all right now, though, aren't you? I mean, *really* all right now?"

"Get my dad, will you? Quickly."

The last two minutes were a mess. Dad burst in. "Ready?"

"I've finished," said Telly. "Get Sam."

"But I thought you were keying Startup."

"No," said Telly. "Sam is."

Everyone had gathered around the cubicle door. Sam Lightfoot was pushed through the crowd with less than a minute to spare. Telly explained in less than ten seconds. Sam glowed. He'd love to. Twenty-eight, twenty-seven, twenty-six counted the onscreen clock.

"Okay," said Dad. "When the clock reaches zero, you key in a single command."

"What's the command?" asked Sam. Twenty, nineteen, eighteen . . .

"Haven't a clue," said Dad. "Telly's choice."

Telly grinned. "Dad let me drop in the code-word. No one knows it but me."

"You better tell me now," said Sam. Twelve, eleven, ten . . .

"I'll whisper it," said Telly.

"Supposing I get it wrong?" panicked Sam.

"You won't get this wrong," said Telly.

. . . seven, six, five . . . Telly whispered. "Got it?"

"Got it."

. . . three, two, one, STARTUP!

Sam Lightfoot keyed in a G. Then an A. Then quickly, an R and a Y. GARY said the screen. GARY said the turbine to all the other turbines. Whenever you're ready, start. GARY GARY GARY.

The tower above them shuddered. Telly looked up. A mighty thrum and a rush—and another. Telly touched the walls. The walls of the tower were alive with a steadily gathering heartbeat. Rush. Thrum. Rush. A whining tone rose somewhere above them in the darkness. Something very big was waking up.

"How does it work?" asked Sam Lightfoot, half-frightened by what he'd started.

"The command you keyed in tells all the turbines to check themselves over and start up whenever they're ready," said Dad, looking up as well. "They should all kick in over the course of the next five minutes or so. The computer in each turbine sends a message which releases the brakes. Then the blades start turning. Once the blades are up to speed, the generator trips in. Hope that new blade behaves itself."

"Come on," said Telly, pushing past, "let's go out and see."

The scene outside was riotous. Telly had to laugh. Ray and Race lit rockets over on the ridge. Anyone who wasn't watching or helping rushed from one tower to another as the blades began to turn, guessing which turbine would be the next one to start, shouting, pointing, looking up, bumping into each other. Those who weren't doing anything else toasted the Startup with cider or anything else they could find. Will Fishbone trained his binoculars on Crossways. Denny tugged for a look. A rocket streaked up from the ridge, blossoming high in the sky over the steadily accelerating blades. And another—and another, and another, exploding in sparkling starbursts. Ray straightened, watching the new blade anxiously. Telly caught his eye. She gave him a joyful thumbs up. The newly installed blade swished around and around with the others, whiter than all the rest. Everything's—*swish*—all right. Ray grinned and waved. Another rocket screamed in the sky, opening like a chrysanthemum, pink and green as the flaming tail of Fleet-Hibble.

Telly joined the rush from one tower to the next. GARY GARY GARY screamed every screen in every shuddering turbine—GARY GARY GARY—like some unstoppable computer virus that infected everything with a self-replicating message that would go on for ever and ever.

"Crossways are go!" Denny waved his binoculars.

Everyone jumped and cheered. Telly remembered Dad's binoculars, forgotten around her neck. Focussing at last on Crossways, she saw that it was true. The not-so-distant stately blades were taking up the rhythm. Eastwards over the moor, Caldicott would be watching for Startup at Crossways—and beyond *that*, Windy Ridge would be watching Caldicott. Beyond Windy Ridge were all the other windfarms waiting for the Startup that would take them wheeling into the twenty-first century.

Telly looked up. It was deeply satisfying to see the blade that had set her on such a strange and purposeful track that night in the storm turning with all the others. It was strange how things had turned out. They hadn't calmed the weather—who could? There would be other welcome lulls like this—and other storms to follow. Instead, they'd calmed themselves. Whatever the challenge in future, they would be more than equal to it. The turbines said it all. Everything—*swish*—goes on. Everything—*swish*—goes on. GARY GARY GARY.

"He was a part of it, wasn't he?" Sam Lightfoot looked up beside her.

"Is," said Telly. *"Is."*

Dad watched Telly watching the turbines. All her friends stood around her. *These kids,* he thought, *they're great. So bright, so aware, so—caring. The future will be safe in their hands.*

"Next century belongs to you lot," he said, suddenly proud to join them. "I've got a feeling you'll all make the best of it."

Telly nodded, watching. The flashing blades tumbled on and on in no particular hurry, strong and clean and right, on and on and on, into the things to come. *Wonderful things,* thought Telly. *The calm after the storm. That's the whole rest of my life. All—however much there is left of it. Here's hoping it's just like today.*